MODOC,
THE LAST SUNDOWN

L. P. HOLMES

SAGEBRUSH
Large Print Westerns

First published in Great Britain by Hale
First published in the United States by Dodd, Mead

First Isis Edition
published 2018
by arrangement with
Golden West Literary Agency

A catalogue record for this book is available
from the British Library.

ISBN 978–1–78541–393–3 (pb)

Published by
F. A. Thorpe (Publishing)
Anstey, Leicestershire

Set by Words & Graphics Ltd.
Anstey, Leicestershire
Printed and bound in Great Britain by
T. J. International Ltd., Padstow, Cornwall

This book is printed on acid-free paper

CHAPTER
ONE

There was a full dozen of them, all armed. Wraithlike, they moved through the chill mists seeping up from the reed- and tule-lined sloughs and ditches which cut twisting furrows across the meadowlands bordering the lake. Clad in the castoffs of the white man, they were ragged and nondescript. Their single common possession was the dread purpose couched in their dark faces and burning in the depths of their black eyes. For in the bitterness of their hearts they were all Modoc warriors, pledged to the ancient cause.

In his main hay meadow, Angus Laird toiled. A big man, lusty of hair and beard, he put the weight of his broad back and heavy shoulders into the laying of the timbers of the stake-and-rider fence he was building around this year's towering stack of winter hay. Last fall he'd neglected such a fence, and through the winter months following, the cattle had fed and burrowed into the stack, undercutting it, and much valuable, hard-won fodder had fallen and been trampled and wasted. This winter, he vowed, that sort of thing wouldn't happen. The cattle would stay outside the fence and feed on what hay was forked over to them.

1

Pausing in his labors to load and light his pipe, Angus looked out across the lake's mist-filmed face, which spread cold and gray under a sunless sky, a sky now etched with endless lines of winging waterfowl. Down they came from somewhere beyond the world's far rim in milling, countless hordes, swarming on the lake waters and along the swampy borders, adding their clamor to that of the teeming thousands already resting there.

This was one of the things about the autumn season which Angus Laird especially liked, this arrival of the clarion-voiced, winged legions from the north. For theirs was the call of all the far-flung skies of the world, and it stirred up the nameless thrill of the primitive in a man.

Now also, Angus reckoned, if the womenfolks, Mary and Lorna, were to have a chance to salt down the usual three or four kegs of fat duck and goose breasts against winter's coming need, then he and Obe had better forget ranch chores for a couple of days and do some shooting. In particular would Obe welcome such a break in the toiling demands of the autumn season.

At thought of Obe, Angus' eyes warmed. It had been right on two years now since young Obe Adams had ridden in at the ranch in search of a strayed horse. He had come in across the Warners with a wagon party, bound for the Oregon country by way of the old Applegate trail. Just turned twenty, lanky and rawboned, with a shock of straw-colored hair, a solid mouth and chin, and a pair of blue eyes that looked at you steady and respectful and didn't miss anything.

Especially not the look and smile of a pretty lass of his own age, like Lorna.

After that it had not taken overly much persuasion to get Obe to forget all about the Oregon country, and to stay on as a ranch hand. A might good one he'd turned out to be, too; none better, in fact. Then, nigh on a year ago, he and Lorna had made a match of it, and now Obe was a son-in-law and a partner. And none better there, either.

These thoughts drew Angus' glance to the south, where Obe was coming upmeadow with a load of fence timbers, the heavy Merivale wagon rolling easy and sure behind the bay team — the big bay team that always moved so steady and powerful. The best team, by God, exulted Angus in a rush of pride, on any ranch along this east shore of Tule Lake!

Turning back to his work, Angus Laird paused, his attention fixed on the angle of a drain ditch some hundred yards distant, where tules and reeds fringed thickly. These had stirred under movement of some sort, and now as he waited and watched, went still again.

He picked up his shovel. Some sort of wild beastie, he decided. Maybe one of those little prairie wolves which men called coyotes. Or a squat badger. Likelier still, perhaps a big old raccoon, of which there were always plenty around, prowling the ditches and sloughs on the hunt.

But now another thought came to Angus Laird, and with it a strange bristling that rippled up his spine, a feeling which surged from nowhere and for no apparent good reason. Yet, abruptly, it was there. And it had him erect and staring when they came lunging out of the ditch and through the tule fringe.

They came at a crouched run, ragged and dirty and fouled to the hips with mud and slime. Their weapons, however, were high and ready, and they covered a good third of the distance between ditch and haystack before the full significance of their dread purpose struck home in Angus Laird's consciousness.

He had no weapon near, save the shovel in his hands. This he swung up, prepared to brain the first of the group to come in reach. And so stood his ground, a brave and prideful man. Yet one surely and pitifully doomed.

When thirty yards away they stopped their rush, and from that distance killed him in a ragged spatter of shots. He had no chance to fight back, no time for even a final thought for Mary — and Lorna — and Obe! Struck in the head and heart, he died instantly, which was well. For when he crumpled down they were at him, clubbing with gun butts, slashing with knives. Then they left him and darted past the haystack and on downmeadow.

Sitting the high seat of the heavy wagon with its load of fence timbers, and rolling along so steadily and surely behind the bay team, Obe Adams had been watching the swarming wildfowl over the lake, though his thoughts were all on Lorna and what she had told him this morning while she lay within the curve of his arm, and the first cold, thin sliver of dawn light seeped into their room.

4

It was, Obe vowed, just about the finest, biggest news that could come to a man, and he was all for jumping out of bed, then and there, and spreading the news at the top of his lungs, so Angus and Mary would know about it, too. But Lorna, laughing softly at such nonsense, had clung to him and wouldn't let him go until he'd promised not to say a word about it before suppertime that evening.

For suppertime, Lorna said, was the good, warm homey time, the right time to talk over all family affairs, such as a baby in the offing. So he'd promised, and he'd keep the promise. Something he'd never do, Obe vowed, was ever to break any promise he made to Lorna. But he sure had near busted at breakfast, trying to act ordinary and easy. And while working all day alongside of Angus, it was going to be mighty hard to keep on acting ordinary and easy.

He wondered how Angus and Mary would be when they got the word at suppertime? Most likely, as women did over such things, Mary would probably talk forty to the dozen, and even cry a little, she'd be so excited and happy. Angus? Well, he'd just lean back and smile some with his lips and a big lot with his eyes, way far back. Angus and Mary were the sort to dote a lot on grandchildren.

A wide-angled vee of honker geese, making an incoming swing toward the lake, sailed overhead, so low that the whistle of their pinions was plain to Obe's ears. Stirred from his thoughts, he looked up at the sliding wedge of the great, majestic birds. And it was at this precise moment that the hard rattle of a ragged volley of gunshots came from farther upmeadow, to jerk both Obe's thoughts and glance down and ahead.

He looked for Angus, who, only a little bit ago, had been standing there by the upreared bulk of the big haystack. But he could see nothing of that sturdy, well-loved figure. All Obe saw now was a huddle of dark-faced, ragged beings, crowding around and hitting at something on the ground. Then, even as he watched and tried to understand, the ragged group broke and came racing toward him.

Obe was still trying to accept the stark reality of what he saw when one of the Modocs, overeager, fired a shot from long range, and the bullet told with a slap against the wagon just under the footboard. It was this fact that stripped aside the last trace of Obe's dazed incredulity.

Full understanding struck home. Brokenly, Obe realized there was nothing he could do for Angus — dreadfully nothing. Those shots — and then the gun butts clubbing at something on the ground. Angus was surely dead, for the Modocs would not have left him, else. And there was nothing you could do for a man already dead. But there was something to be done for Lorna and Mary!

A second bullet slammed into the wagon, and a third snapped past Obe's head, very close. Yelling and using the whip, he hauled the big team around in a sharp swing to the left. If he could just make it back to the house in time to warn Lorna and Mary, to get them safely behind barred doors. Then, with Angus' rifle and his own, and the women loading for him, maybe he could make a good fight of it.

It wasn't often that the big bay team felt the bite of the whip. Now, when they did, they broke into a heavy trot, heads tossing, bringing the wagon around, skidding and lurching. They were almost through the swing, almost straightened out for home, when a leaden hornet, buzzing in from a Modoc gun, nipped the off horse across the flank. Not a serious wound, but one biting deep enough to bring a little blood filming down the glossy hide. And stinging, sending the animal into a ponderous gallop that lifted its companion in harness to a matching gait.

Powerfully they ran, their pounding hoofs chopping up and scattering gouts of meadow sod, while the heavily loaded wagon rocked and careened behind them. They ran with heads outthrust, with nostrils distended, gripped now in some wild frenzy of their own. They ran well, the big bays did, massively and surely.

But there was a Modoc warrior who ran well, too; who ran like a vengeful, hunting wolf. He gained to within fair distance of the wagon, then dropped to one knee and aimed with sinister care. Powder smoke mushroomed and the gun report fluttered soddenly across the meadowland. Shot through and through between the shoulders, Obe Adams fell forward off the wagon seat and hung limp across the footboard. The reins slid from his fingers, trailed at the heels of the team. And the big bays pounded on . . .

Mary Laird was out by the bench at the corner of the woodshed, leeching wood ashes. She was a big woman, solidly boned, grown heavy about the hips. Of pioneer stock she had been a true and good wife and mother, and there was the patience and courage of her kind reflected in her fine, strong-featured face. Against morning's dank chill she had wrapped a shawl about her head, and over her one-piece, full-length calico dress wore one of her husband's old coats.

A vagrant wind had begun to move out of the west, puffing strongly up one moment, dwindling the next, and it brought the clamor of the wildfowl from the lake as an uneven, up-and-down cadence of sound. One moment it would be a swelling tumult, dwarfing all else, the next it would fade to a murmuring, but persistent undertone. Against this rise and fall, other sounds were muffled and confused, stripped of their true significance.

So it was that the snap and snarl of gunfire never did reach Mary Laird's ears with any meaning, and the heavy pound of running hoofs did not fully register and bring her around and wondering until the bay team and the wagon were less than a hundred yards of the corral.

Now, as she watched them come on, her first thought was that the bays had merely seized a chance to break for home, with no harm done other than to leave Angus and Obe afoot up in the hay meadow. On second thought, however, she decided this was unlikely, for more than once had Angus told her, while bragging about the big bay team, that they were the steadiest, most reliable pair of horses he'd ever owned.

The bays wheeled through a short half swing and pulled to a gusty, snorting halt at the corral gate. And it was as the wagon came around to this new angle that

Mary Laird saw the limp figure crumpled across the footboard and balanced so precariously there. Slowly, stiffly, she walked over, a freezing fear clutching at her heart.

Behind her the kitchen door opened and slammed shut again as Lorna came out, drawn by the ponderous, rushing arrival of the big team. Lorna called anxiously, but Mary Laird neither answered nor looked back. Because she had no words at the moment, and because she wasn't sure about Obe — and she had to be sure! Lorna, running after her, called again, anxiety shrilling her voice to a wail.

"Obe! Obe —!"

When the team made that heavy, sliding stop, there at the corral gate, the wagon had crowded up on them, and this the bays did not like. So now, of their own accord, they laid the weight and power of their broad haunches against the breeching, and with a lunge, backed the wagon up a yard or two. This abrupt rearward jerk unbalanced Obe's limp body and dropped it from the footboard down across the wagon tongue and from there to the ground, fairly under the rear hoofs of the team.

The big bays cowered and cringed, yet stood stock-still when Mary Laird, bending and reaching, got hold of Obe and dragged him clear. When she did this, she knew what she had to know. Obe was dead.

Lorna knew it, too, knew it the moment she touched the gaunt, still figure of her boyish husband. She called his name in a thin little moan. Then she was crouching, kneeling, huddling, gathering Obe's head and shoulders into her arms, and the tragedy of her sobbing was a scar across all reason.

Mary Laird looked down at them, at the two who had been hers. But only one, now — only one —

And Angus? What about Angus? Oh, dear God, what of Angus!

At first she walked, crying his name. Then she began to run, up the far length of the hay meadow. She ran awkwardly and heavily, for the easy grace of her girlhood was long gone, and the bulky flesh about her hips was a jouncing, unwieldy weight. Yet she ran, numbed with dread, her heart pounding, her breath raw and choking in her throat.

Up in the meadow she met them, the full dozen of them, darkly fierce of eye and face, and she fully expected them to strike her dead. Instead, they merely stood and watched her and made no move to lay a hand on her.

But as she passed them, still crying for Angus, guttural words in broken English followed her.

"We are Modoc. You are safe from us. Only the white man shoots squaw!"

They went on then, past the corral, past the huddled figure of Lorna, who, in her black pit of heartbreak and stricken grief, neither saw nor heard them. One or two began edging toward the ranch house, intent on loot, but harsh command by their scarfaced leader brought them back into line. For there were more ranches to strike at, where more deadly business could be done if no warning or alarm had time to reach ahead.

So it was that they caught George Roblett and his two stalwart sons knee-deep in the mud of a drain ditch they were deepening. Standing on the bank above the three men, the Modocs fired almost straight down on them, and so killed them and left them there, crumpled in the cold, lifeless mud.

Still farther south along the lake shore they surprised Pete Thurman and his hired man, Nick Dutra, cutting wood against winter's coming need, and shot them down within calling distance of the Thurman ranch house.

Now the raiders swung away from the lake somewhat, heading for the Hume ranch, back where the land climbed above the flatness of the lake-shore meadows. Back where the gray sagebrush clothed the slopes, where the darker gray-green of juniper and mahogany thickets filled winding gulches, and the quaking aspens and the cherry brush built pockets of gold and warm crimson under the run of the rimrocks.

On one of the sage slopes, one of John Hume's riders, Neale Bender, met with the ominous dozen. This time surprise was mutual, and Bender, desperately hauling his mount around and spurring for cover, made it safely ahead of the hasty shots sent after him. They tried pursuit for a little way, but Bender raced quickly out of range.

With Bender carrying the alarm, the Modocs knew there was no chance of surprising the Hume ranch as they had the others. They knew also that soon armed and vengeful men would be looking for them; mounted men, capable of running them down in any sort of open country.

They would have liked to go on, for their blood was hot, their defiant ferocity unappeased. But it was not well to ask too much of the gods on this gray December day in 1872. So they angled back toward the lake shore, there to disappear into the vast, far-running mat of tule growth, through which they worked their way steadily to the south toward the distant lift of a land of lava, showing dark and cold under the day's somber mantle.

For the decision had been made, the last trail charted, and somewhere in those dim, savage lavas the final destiny of all Modoc men would be fulfilled.

CHAPTER
TWO

With a pack mule and extra horse at lead, Ward Sebastian rode up to the Dutra cabin through a cold, blue dusk. There was a thin glow of light in the lone window of the place which served to emphasize, rather than diminish its forlorn loneliness.

Sebastian knew a bleak distaste of the errand that had brought him here, but he had faced worse things this tragic day, so now he dismounted, moved to the cabin door and knocked. There was an inner stir, then a woman's voice, calling.

"Nick?"

"No, Kitty. Ward Sebastian."

Sounded the scrape of a bar being withdrawn, and then the door opened and let a gush of light strike his grave face and spare, square-shouldered figure. Kitty Dutra exclaimed.

"Ward! Come in!"

He entered, then stood for a quiet moment, his glance running over the meager limits of the cabin's single room, while he searched for the gentlest way he knew to frame the words he had to speak.

At his elbow, Kitty Dutra noted his restless glance and misunderstood it. She flicked an indicating hand at the barren poverty of the place and spoke with a hard cynicism.

"You've never seen the inside of this place before, have you, Ward? Well, it's probably as good as I deserve. But please, no pity from you."

Looking down at her he saw the same dusky intensity in her that she'd possessed in the old days when she was Kitty McCloud. Also, he thought, much of the challenging beauty of those days was still there. He drew a deep breath and made the plunge in the only way he could, which was directly.

"You always did have courage, so I know you'll show it now. Maybe there is some other and better way to say this, but I can't think of it. Kitty — Nick is gone."

"Gone! What do you mean? You — Oh —!" She went very still, staring at him. Her voice dropped low.

"Ward, you're telling me that Nick is — dead?"

He nodded gravely.

"A Modoc raiding party. He wasn't alone. They got Pete Thurman at the same time. They had already done for Angus Laird and Obe Adams, and for George Roblett and his two boys. I couldn't think of anything to say to the womenfolk of those men, and I can't think of anything to say to you. Except that it's been one hell of a rough day for a lot of people."

She turned half away, looking straight ahead, her eyes wide and unseeing. Presently, in that same low, hushed tone, she asked:

"Where is he?"

"We buried him with Pete Thurman on the slope above the Thurman ranch house. Jack Hume, two of his

14

men, Sam Lester and I took care of that. We did the same for the rest of the poor, unfortunate devils, and we had to be quick about it, for there were the womenfolks and their necessary belongings to be moved to Jack Hume's place, where they'll be safe. Now I've come after you."

"You'd take me somewhere?"

"Yes. For the present, to my ranch. I got a mule outside for your gear, and a horse for you to ride. I sent Sam Lester on ahead with the pack string."

If I keep on talking of practical things, he thought, maybe she won't go to pieces like a couple of the others did.

Kitty Dutra showed no sign of going to pieces. Instead, she moved over to the window and stood there with her back to him. And when she spoke, her voice was again level and strong.

"Don't wait for me to start crying, Ward. I'm not going to. Perhaps I've been a fool in many ways, but never a hypocrite. You see, I've long since done my weeping. Oh, I'm not blaming Nick for a single thing, understand. But there's been nothing between him and me for a long time, and there never was anything really solid or worthwhile there. Now, Nick is gone. If it does any good to be sorry, then I'm truly, truly sorry for him. But I'm done with weeping." She was silent for a moment, then added, "I can't go with you, Ward. I'll stay here."

"No," he told her bluntly, "you won't. Get your gear together."

She shook her head. "You've done far too much for the McCloud family already. When I think of all you did for my father, for that worthless brother of mine! And what thanks did you ever get?"

"None of which has a damned thing to do with my taking you with me," said Sebastian gruffly. "You know you can't stay here alone from now on."

"Neither can I stay at your ranch," she retorted. "So —!"

"So you're coming along and no more nonsense. You can stay on until you get a straight trail for the future figured out."

She came around to face him, studying him intently. "If I could just be sure it wasn't pity — ?"

"Pity! What the devil has pity got to do with it? A Modoc raid made a widow out of you. And like always, when open Indian trouble breaks, the white renegades start prowling, figuring that any shady business they might stir up, will be blamed on the Modocs. You're a lone woman, way off by yourself. And you can't stay here. That's final!"

Abruptly she was agreeable. She moved swiftly, making up a big bundle of her things. A coffeepot simmered on the stove. Sebastian poured a cup for her and one for himself. As she drank, she swung her glance in a final survey of the cabin. After which she turned with a gust of the old, fierce intensity.

"I said I wasn't a hypocrite, didn't I? Well, now for some more truth. I've hated this place, Ward. You've no idea how long and how much. I never want to see it again! Does that make me heartless — or callous?"

"Of course not." His tone gentled, and he looked at her with real sympathy in his eyes. "You've had it pretty rough in a lot of ways, haven't you?"

She turned away quickly.

"A little of that kind of talk and I'll be weeping. I'm not exactly used to kindness, you know. Let's get out of here."

They rode the miles and the hours down through a night that pressed close in all its wild blackness. It was the sort of night when all the fears and specters of man's most primitive heritage might rise to haunt him, and it seemed to Kitty Dutra that these things were all about them in the chill mists.

It was a full half hour after midnight when they reined in at Sebastian's headquarters, to find lights still burning and people waiting for them. Sam Lester and old Bob Gayle came to take over the horses and the pack mule. Sebastian chided them gruffly.

"No need of this. You two should be in bed. Sam, you know we pull out for Yreka early."

"Yeah," said Sam, "I know. But if you can miss sleep, then I can. After you get Mrs. Dutra settled, Bob's got some news for you."

Shouldering Kitty Dutra's bundle of gear, Sebastian led her into the ranch house. Here Bob Gayle's wife, white-haired and kindly, was waiting. When she put a welcoming and understanding arm about Kitty Dutra's shoulders, there showed another crack in that bitter-hard armor. Kitty's lips trembled and a swift rush of moisture glistened in her eyes.

Sebastian left the women alone and went out to the bunkhouse. The stove was purring with heat and he backed up to it, his hands spread behind him, his shoulders sagging under the pull of fatigue.

Standing so, he was a man with the limber-lean flanks, the narrow hips and wiry, hard-muscled legs of one much in the saddle. Whisker stubble smudged a jaw line tight drawn near to gauntness. Under a high-bridged nose his mouth was clean lipped, bracketed just now with lines of weariness and regret. His deep-blue eyes were dulled a trifle by that same inner shadow. Now, as Sam Lester and Bob Gayle came in, he put his glance on them.

"All right, Bob, you got something to tell me?"

The old rider nodded. "Two, three things. First off, you're minus a hand. Chumlucky Pete, he's lit out. Night before last, he's here, same as usual. Next morning he's gone. I don't know why, I don't know where."

Sebastian, brooding, nodded slowly. "I think I do. What else, Bob?"

"Yesterday afternoon I took a ride out through the mahogany brakes past Lost Horse Rim, like you told me to. We got some cattle out there, but not as many as we did by at least half-a-dozen head, for I found what was left of six of them, which wasn't much. They'd been fresh slaughtered."

"You mean — slow-elked?"

"That's right. Haunches, loins and shoulders had been cut out. Who do you think? The military, maybe?"

Sebastian shook his head. "Not the military."

"Who, then?"

"Captain Jack's people, probably. The Modocs."

A flash of anger showed in Bob Gayle's eyes.

"Scurvy devils!" he exclaimed. "Treatin' us so, after all we done for them in the past. Chumlucky Pete would have known right where to find the cattle. Likely he was in on the slaughterin'."

"Likely," nodded Sebastian.

"Damned thievin', scurvy devils!" said old Bob again.

"Easy to say, Bob — but maybe not fair. For the rules work both ways."

"Rules of what?"

"War," said Sebastian. "And that's what this is."

The old rider considered for a little time, then shrugged.

"Reckon you're right. Speakin' of such, an officer and a couple of troopers were by today. Looked everything over real sharp and important. I braced 'em to see what about. Officer said they might have to quarter troops here, same as they have at Frank Searchly's and Henry Gallatin's. I told him he'd have to see you to get permission, and he said he didn't need permission. A real smart bucko. I felt like cuffin' him."

The ghost of a smile touched Sebastian's lips. Bob Gayle and his wife had been with the ranch for a long time. Both were fiercely loyal.

"If the military wants to move in on us, Bob, they'll move in," Sebastian said. "And there's nothing we can do about it." He yawned until his jaws cracked, then stared straight ahead at nothing as he somberly added: "Things are happening in this damned world there's just no good answer to. I've seen my share of such in the last couple of days. I hope I never have to go through anything like it again, though I'm afraid I will."

"Now," said Sam Lester, "I know what you mean. That buryin' chore was bad enough, but it was them poor heartbroke womenfolks who pulled me to pieces inside. Still and all, I've listened to Modoc squaws wailin' their dead, too. I guess human tears don't belong to one side any more than they do the other. Well, boy, we'd best turn in. We got only four or five hours before we head out again."

Sebastian nodded, taking off his coat and moving toward a bunk. Outside, a thin, cold rain began to drift down out of the Stygian sky.

Past the ears of his horse, Ward Sebastian watched the trail lead from the dripping junipers and mahoganies of the higher ground down the twisting run of a gulch which presently met the open of a long sagebrush flat curving past the north shoulder of Sheet Iron Butte. Here the gulch discharged a shallow spread of storm water, and when Sebastian's mount went through it with jogging hoofs, a thin boil of muddy foam beat up.

Close behind, the mules of the pack string swung to the pace, their heads low against the misty drive of the rain that had been falling since before dawn light of this wintry, northern California day. Two of the mules carried meager loads of camp gear, but the sawbuck saddles of the rest were empty save for folded tarpaulin and coiled rope. Back in the drag of the string, Sam

20

Lester rode as a humped, rain-blurred figure in his old buffalo coat.

A high, slightly forward leaning figure in the saddle, lean cheeks whipped to near numbness by the ceaseless pelt of the cold rain, Sebastian stoically endured the misery and monotony of these long, storm-beaten miles. Now, approaching Sheet Iron, he marked the outline of the dark, lava-crusted mass with a single fleeting glance, seeing it merely as something that indicated distance traveled and distance still to go. Then he faced ahead once more and frowned into the grim shadow of his thoughts.

Some of these carried the weight of time on them, others the burden of but a few short days. And in none could he find comfort. For in all, framed beyond forgetting, lay pictures of terror and misery and death; pictures indelibly stained by blood already shed and tears already wept by both white man and red, with more of each certain to come.

For the military was gathering and massing weight along the west shore of Tule Lake, with all signs pointing to the fact that the Modocs were forting up in the wild lavas south of the lake, defying the white man to drive them out.

This stand was not the defiant, impulsive decision of a moment. Rather, there was an inevitability about it, the sure culmination of years of worsening conditions in just one more phase of the same sad, blood-stained, miserable conflict that had accompanied the white man on his march of conquest all across a continent.

Also, Sebastian mused bleakly, it was in large part the same old and shameful story of lies and deceit, of peace talks so insincere they could never bring true peace, of promises glibly made and callously broken, of political chicanery and cowardice, of greed and duplicity and cruelty and savagery, with now at long last the final bitter tragedy of a people fighting hopelessly against impossible odds, while being driven inexorably into the twilight of their existence.

The end result was, of course, certain. Here, as along all the rest of that weary, bloody trail from East to West, the red man would fight as best he could, for as long as he could, in the only way he knew how. Then he would move on into the shadow land of the last sundown, to join his brothers waiting there.

Prodded by the somberness of these thoughts, made restless and uneasy by the irony of divided sympathies, Ward Sebastian twisted and swung in his saddle. The move saved his life, for instead of smashing into his chest, the bullet was a slicing knife of fire across his left arm, halfway between shoulder and elbow. It was as if an invisible hand had reached out and struck him sharply. Right after, there was the thud of gun report, dulled and muted by the storm, with the echo thinning off into quick nothingness.

In its suddenness, it was a thing to numb a man momentarily. Then, with equal swiftness came reaction, and Sebastian spun his horse in a short swing to the right and back, putting some of the leading pack animals between him and the source of the shot. This, as nearly as he could judge, was a ragged scatter of lava boulders piled at the base of the butte. A moment later he was certain, for before it could be raveled by the rain, a faint drift of powder smoke showed.

Sebastian caught at the butt of the rifle scabbarded under his stirrup leather, and for a desperate moment the weapon hung up in its rain-soaked boot. As he tugged to free it, report and powder smoke spouted from the boulders again. Lead told on flesh with a wicked thud and the mule directly in front of him grunted, humped, made a floundering jump or two, then went down in a rolling heap, legs flailing the air wildly.

Sebastian had no idea who it was skulking out there in the boulders, but of one thing he was certain: so long as they were sheltered and he in the open, the end was sure and certain and in no way to his benefit. So, as he saw it, there was but one move for him to make, and that was the bold and reckless one.

Thus decided, he freed his rifle with a final jerk, spurred clear of the pack mules and drove straight for the boulder pile, swinging rifle to shoulder as he went, knowing a swift gust of thankfulness when he found his left arm answering to his will. It was numb and weighted and shaky, but it was useful. And by this fact he knew that no bone was broken.

He glimpsed a flicker of movement and threw a quick shot, hoping only to unsettle and confuse, rather than with any real expectation of hitting. In this gamble he found some success, for an answering shot flew high and wild. Then it was Sam Lester, spurring up from the drag with an enraged yell and throwing a slug which bounced off a boulder in wailing ricochet. Swiftly, Sam shot again, and again the banshee snarl of glancing lead echoed.

This reckless, vengeful reaction got the calculated result. A crouched figure ducked clear of the lava tangle, racing up and around the shoulder of the butte. Swinging the lever of his Henry, Sebastian tried a shot, but missed widely. Then, realizing the extreme chanciness of getting a hit from the saddle of a speeding horse, he hauled to a stop and levered home another cartridge.

It was still very tough shooting, with the odds all against him. His horse, stung from the spurring, kept swinging and trampling, while the rain whipped him across the eyes and blurred the gun sights. Also, that wounded left arm, while usable, was anything but a firm support for a leveled rifle. Still, out of it all came a fractional moment when the gun lay roughly on the scrambling, storm-dimmed target. At the shot the running figure stumbled went to one knee, then was swiftly up again and limping from sight.

Any attempt to put a horse at speed across the talus slide between the boulder pile and the shoulder of Sheet Iron Butte, was to surely invite a broken leg for the horse and a broken neck for the rider. So Sebastian spurred the longer way around the outer edge of the clutter, and it was here that Sam Lester caught up with him.

"Where?" demanded Sam.

Sebastian pointed with the barrel of his rifle. Even as he did so, a rider, flattened far out along the neck of his speeding horse, flashed through the gap between the butte and rim of higher country beyond and gained sure sanctuary there. Distance, the day's gray, rain-thickened murk, made any sort of identification as impossible as was hope of successful pursuit.

"No use," said Sebastian. "We couldn't come up with him."

Grizzled Sam Lester's face was thin-drawn with anger.

"If I could have got just one clean try at him! But I see a look about you. He nicked you somewhere, didn't he?"

Sebastian scabbarded his rifle, then felt his left arm. The sleeve of his coat was becoming soggy with something besides rain. The first numbness was leaving and the throb of a settled pain taking over.

"He got hold of me a little," Sebastian admitted. "As I'm sure I did him. He stumbled at my last shot and was limping when he went on."

Down along the flat where several massive boulders of black lava broke the slanting drive of the rain, Sebastian dismounted and peeled off his coat. The heavy wool of his shirt sleeve was too bulky to roll back enough to bare the wound entirely, so the best they could do was to have Sam Lester knot a bandanna tightly into place over sleeve and all.

"Not a very fancy job," Sam said as he helped Sebastian into his coat again. "You got any ideas of who?"

Sebastian shook his head. "I'd be guessing. But like I said, I marked him. I'll be looking for somebody with a limp."

"Well, now," said Sam grimly, "So will I!"

They rode back to the mule that had gone down. It was still alive, but there was no hope for it. Sober regret in his eyes, Sam Lester leveled his rifle and the report thumped soddenly. After which he stripped all gear from the dead animal and loaded it on another of the pack string. Climbing stiffly back into his saddle, he made growling comment.

"Just in case there's another damned skulker around with a loose trigger finger, it's my turn to qualify as the target. I'm pointing the string from here on in."

The mules had bunched up, but soon they were lined out again, picking up their trail covering pace, which, under empty saddles, was half-jog, half-fast, swinging walk. At the rear of the string, Ward Sebastian looped reins about the saddle horn, folded his left arm across his body and supported it with his right hand cupped under the elbow, thus easing the pull of pain somewhat.

Ahead, before he could find shelter and comfort, lay hours of time and long miles of distance, with no possible way of compressing either. There was nothing a man could do other than accept these facts and make the best of them. So he tipped his head against the drive of the rain and set himself to ride it out, once more donning a cloak of locked-away stoicism. As he rode he turned dark speculation over and over in his mind. Who? And why?

CHAPTER
THREE

By the time the pack string reached and headed up the curving run of Shasta Valley, the darkness of day's end was closing in. The rain had slackened, but now mules and men moved into a thickening land fog which swirled and scudded before a wind driving down from the Siskiyou Mountains, bringing with it the wet pungency of drenched conifer timber, and the biting chill of not too distant snow slopes. Nearing the end of the trip and on familiar ground, the mules quickened their pace and Sam Lester pulled aside to let them pass, then dropped in beside Ward Sebastian, staring narrowly at him through the frigid twilight.

"How's that arm?"

Straightening under the soggy weight of his storm-drenched coat, Sebastian carefully eased his stiffened shoulders with a flexing roll. His lips pulled wryly.

"Not too bad. But I'm damned glad we're getting close to town."

"Just so," said Sam, wagging his head. He straightened and stared ahead. "Now what the hell —?"

A thinly yellow glow had resolved through the misty dusk. A heavy voice lifted profanely and the pack mules slowed and began to bunch up. Sebastian and Sam swung wide and spurred up past them.

Here were tents and men in uniform, and several campfires hissing and smoking sourly in the wetness. Blocked off by this camp set squarely across the trail, the mules were beginning to mill uncertainly. A trooper advanced on them, cursing and waving a length of firewood.

Sebastian hit him with curt words. "Easy there — easy!"

Thick-set, and wearing a sergeant's stripes, the trooper faced about belligerently.

"Your mules?"

"Obvious, isn't it?"

"Then get them out of here! Where's your sense, driving into this camp?"

Crusty Sam Lester leaned truculently forward in his saddle, a growl in his throat.

"Ah, these sergeants! Times I doubt I'll ever get used to the breed. Like now. Speaking of sense, soldier, where's yours, pitching your damned camp across a main-traveled trail?"

Before the sergeant could answer, a young officer in a long military overcoat came briskly in past the tents.

"What's the trouble, Grimes? These mules —?"

"Theirs, sir." The sergeant indicated Sebastian and Sam Lester. "And I was —"

"The mules," cut in Sebastian, "were heading for Yreka along a trail they've traveled a hundred times

28

before. They come up against a camp set across the trail. Who's to blame?"

Meeting Sebastian's glance for a grave moment, the young officer flushed, then answered quietly.

"When you put it that way, I am. Daylight was running out and I had to get my men under cover. Other outfits had already taken up the better locations. I had no time to pick and choose."

The glow of the nearest fire was weak and uncertain, yet it reached far enough to touch the face of the officer and show a pair of steady eyes and a set of clean-cut, sensitive features, whipped to ruddiness by the wind's raw breath. The faint lift of anger that had begun to stir in Sebastian, faded out.

"Fair enough," he conceded. "I can see how that would be. We could have been more alert. But we're just in from Tule Lake and the last time we were through, the trail was open."

Swift interest gleamed in the young lieutenant's eyes. "Tule Lake! Anywhere near the active area?"

"Near enough."

"What's the word? Here the talk has it that the latest peace effort was unsuccessful. Which could be rumor, of course."

"No rumor," Sebastian said. "The peace palaver at Natural Bridge exploded in gunsmoke."

"There's been further fighting?"

"A little. Modoc raids have hit some civilians pretty savage. But the real showdown hasn't started yet."

"You believe then that this Modoc chief, this Captain Jack as he is called, will attempt to make a stand of it?"

Sebastian stirred in his saddle. Impatience lifted in him. How unrealistic in their damned professional smugness could some of the military be? Well, they had things to learn and learn them they would, and the lesson would be written savagely in pain and blood.

"Lieutenant," he said, tersely dry. "That you may surely depend on. Captain Jack will make a stand of it."

Grimes, the sergeant, spoke with a swagger.

"If he does, it will soon be done. He'll find the Regulars a different breed than the state militia recruits, or some ragtag bunch of civilian volunteers."

Sam Lester, head tipped against the bitter drive of the wind, looked Grimes up and down, spat, then made growling, sardonic comment.

"Will he now! My fine bucko friend, when this thing really starts, and you've had your stupid ears whipped off half a dozen times, then if you still be alive and I come across you, I'll remind you of that little brag!"

Saying which, Sam stirred his mount and began working the pack string clear of camp. Sebastian reined to help him. The lieutenant called after them.

"Better swing wide. A lot of picket lines between here and Yreka —!"

It took a full half-hour to cover the final mile through the bitterly cold, ever-thickening gloom. On all sides, it seemed, lines of tents were pitched under the scattered valley timber. A dozen times the pack string was challenged, and twice that many times it was well cursed by fatigue details of one sort and another that it ran foul of.

30

Everywhere lifted the drone of occupation, the multitude of sounds given off by many men at many duties. Campfires fought wet fuel and laid an acrid, eye-stinging smoke across the world, to mix with and thicken the fog mists. The lone relieving note, Sebastian decided, was the good fragrance of cooking coffee, which lifted here and there to sharpen the bite of his own insistent hunger.

The final limits of the military encampment stopped short of the town of Yreka by some quarter of a mile, and when the harried pack mules finally reached this open area, impatience for quarters sent them at a gear rattling run, and Sebastian and Sam Lester had to spur out ahead to slow the string and bring it safely in at Dan Orcutt's big corral and spread of feed sheds at the foot of Oregon Street. Here was further press and confusion, with Orcutt's voice lifting impatiently.

"I tell you, Holt, I can't do anything for you. The military has taken every extra spear of feed I could spare. And I got to be ready to take care of any of Jeff Chesbro's outfits, or of Ward Sebastian and his string, at all times. For they are regulars with me and depend on me. Sorry, but that's the way it is!"

Leaving Sam Lester to hold back the mules, Sebastian pushed ahead and met up with a tangle of pack animals massed before the corral gate. He sent out a reaching call.

"Ho, Dan! Sebastian, here. Got my string coming in."

Orcutt's reply was swift.

"Ward! Hold off for a little. Holt, right there is what I've been trying to tell you. Get your outfit clear!"

There was a small pause, then came Provo Holt's tight and angry reaction.

"This I'll remember, Orcutt. And maybe at a time when you'll be wishing I'd forgotten. All right, McCloud, move 'em out! We got to hunt other quarters."

In the gloom not far from Sebastian there sounded a dull and weary cursing, and the jam of pack animals about the corral gate began to shift and angle away before the authority of a hard-swung rope end. Abruptly a slash of this whistled by Sebastian, barely missing him. He called curt warning.

"Watch yourself, Yance! It's dark, but not that dark."

At the other end of that swinging rope was Yance McCloud, Kitty Dutra's brother. Sebastian spoke again.

"You're riding in damned poor company, Yance."

His answer to this was another cut of the rope and this time it spatted across his shoulders, the impact solid and hurting, even through the thickness of his heavy, blanket-lined coat. Edgy from fatigue and pain and harsh memories, he knew a fresh gust of bitter anger.

He sent his horse sharply ahead, broke through the press round about, and had a mounted figure in front of him. The rope end was swinging again, but this time he was well inside the arc of it and it wrapped harmlessly about his shoulders. Standing high in his stirrups, he threw his anger into the drive of his right fist.

His target was just a dark and moving blur, but the blow landed solidly and the surly cursing that had been going on, broke abruptly off. Yance McCloud, reeling in his saddle, swung wide as he fought to regain his balance, and when he did so he ducked low along his mount's neck and spurred into the clear.

Another rider moved even with Sebastian, driving the remainder of the pack animals ahead of him. Though just a shadow in the gloom, there was, thought Sebastian bleakly, no mistaking Provo Holt. For, when you utterly despised a man, and he in turn hated you fanatically, then there was no need to see clearly to know recognition. Invisible currents of feeling like these could be as certain as sight or sound.

Provo Holt would have ridden by in silence, but Sebastian tossed a question that was a curt challenge.

"You have a man anywhere in the neighborhood of Sheet Iron Butte today, Holt?"

Holt only partially reined up. "If I did, that would be my business and none of yours."

"Don't be too sure of that. I could be wondering about Jake Ruby."

"What about Jake Ruby?" Provo Holt kept his horse sidling along.

"This!" said Sebastian. "When you see him again, and if he's limping, tell him he better head across the mountains, for good! Because I'll be looking for him. If he's limping, mind you!"

To this, Provo Holt gave no further answer, and his restless horse carried him on into the night, leaving behind only the raw impact of a bitter hatred.

With Holt's outfit clear, Sebastian called in Sam Lester. The mules splashed across the corral muck and into the line of feed sheds at the far end. A couple of Dan Orcutt's roustabouts had come with lanterns to help with the unsaddling chore.

"You," Sam Lester told Sebastian, "stay clear of this and rest that arm. Probably you should get right uptown and have it looked after."

"Not that bad," Sebastian said. "I'll wait for you."

He moved to one side with his rifle and saddlebags and laid them down. He fumbled under his coat for his pipe and sucked absently at its dry emptiness. After all-day exposure to the storm, here in the feed shed out of the wet and direct drive of the wind, it seemed almost warm, and the final embers of anger over the rope-end episode dulled and burned out before the pure pleasure of complete relaxation and physical let-down at the end of a long and wearying trip.

At this moment, Sebastian thoroughly understood a pack animal's skin-loosening shake and gusty snort of relief when free of saddle and cinch and soggy blanket, and then its pushing eagerness for a manger filled with wild timothy. The fundamentals of life, he mused, were really very simple. After exposure, shelter; after hunger, food; after labor, rest.

The animals cared for, Dan Orcutt and his two men went off about other chores. Sebastian and Sam Lester stood for a little time under the wide overhang of the feed shed, reluctant to move again into the full, dank chill of the night.

"Not having cat eyes," said Sam, "I couldn't see that far in the dark. But I heard Yance McCloud cussin' and I heard you warn him about something. Right after which, he quit his cussin' sudden as though his wind pipe had been cut. Anything happen out there by the corral gate I should know about?"

Sebastian told it briefly. "So, when he took another cut with the rope and reached me, I bounced my knuckles off his teeth."

"He's become a surly dog," Sam growled. "He hit the bad arm?"

Sebastian's fingers explored gingerly. "Never touched it. Lucky for me. Lucky for him, too, maybe." He gathered up saddlebags and rifle. "Let's get along."

They went up Oregon Street which, in spite of the night, the raw wind and the sleety rain which had begun to fall again, seethed with activity. Heavy freight and supply wagons, soggy canvas tops drumming in the wind, lumbered by. Men, many of them in uniform, crowded both sides of the street, a restless tide flowing back and forth, in and out of doors, careless of weather, stirred and driven by the excitement that has no equal in the lives of mortals — the dread excitement of war, or promise of it!

Working their way through the crush, Sam Lester made sarcastic comment.

"If it takes all these goings on by the military, along with what they already got scattered around back at the lake, just to corral Captain Jack and mebbe fifty, sixty

35

Modoc braves, then, as one of these here noble palefaces I figger I got damned little to brag about. Matter of fact, I'm getting smaller by the minute."

Sebastian smiled faintly. "Like Henry Gallatin and Frank Searchly and a few others, you and I see more than one side to the picture."

At the junction of Oregon and Miner Streets, they parted, Sam offering a final word of concern.

"First thing you do, get that arm looked after."

Sebastian said, "Sure. See you tomorrow."

Sam went along to Molly MacGruder's boardinghouse, farther up Oregon. This was home to him and other packers and teamsters while in this town of Yreka. Sebastian turned down Miner to a big, square building with a galleried porch reaching all across the front of it. Here were several windows glowing with light, and a wide door beneath a sign which read:

JEFFERSON CHESBRO. MDSE & SUPPLIES
PACKING CONTRACTED FOR.

Sebastian climbed the porch steps, paused short of the door to shake the worst of the wet from himself. The thickening drive of the rain was a steady drumming on the porch roof, and beyond, where the light of the windows reached, it was a slanting, glittering curtain. Abruptly this curtain parted and two hurrying figures climbed to the shelter of the porch. A girl's bright and breathless laughter lifted, followed by a man's wry comment.

"This may be all stirring adventure to you, Connie, but for me I can see little ahead except a lot of discomfort in a world filled with very foul weather."

The girl laughed again. "Wasn't it field duty both you and Phil were howling for, Jud? Don't tell me you're losing your taste for it already!"

"I can't speak for your brother Phil," was her companion's dry response, "but where I'm concerned, let's say it's my taste for this kind of weather that is wearing thin."

The pair of them crossed through the light flare of a window, and Sebastian saw that the man was military, an officer by the shoulder tabs on his overcoat. The girl was muffled in a dark-blue, ankle-length cloak with an attached hood, and now, sheltered from the wet, she threw this back, disclosing a wealth of storm tousled hair, flashing eyes and cheeks whipped to a vigorous color by wind and rain.

Ward Sebastian followed them into the big combined store and trading post, and at the near end of the counter, laid down his rifle and saddlebags. Several customers were lined at the counter and old Ben Stiles had left his high stool and ledger desk to help Jeff Chesbro take care of them. The officer and the girl paused a little apart, waiting their turn.

Sebastian shrugged out of his coat, drawing a long breath of relief when finally free of its weight. In maneuvering his left arm he worked with care. Even so, his lips tightened under the bite of a sudden twinge of pain. Now, with bent head and carefully probing fingers, he explored the twisted bandanna which bandaged the arm. Both it and the sleeve of his shirt were clotted and stiffened with dried blood.

He lifted his head to find the girl in the cloak watching him. Her glance was impersonal, yet charged with open interest as it touched the rifle and saddlebags on the counter, moved to the holstered belt gun strapped about his narrow flanks, then took note of his bandaged arm before lifting to his face. It was a gray-eyed glance, very clear, which held his own steadily, neither boldly forward or coquettishly shy, just unaffectedly bright and wondering.

Beyond the end of the counter a door opened and Helen Chesbro came in. A slender woman, she was plain of face until she smiled, when she was transformed completely. She exclaimed at sight of Sebastian.

"Ward! Safely with us again! You'll never know how you worry Jeff and me."

Genuinely fond of this woman, the pull of harshness on Sebastian's face softened under the warmth of her greeting. He showed her a twisted grin.

"Never worry about me, Helen. I'll always be underfoot."

Now she discovered the blood-crusted bandage and caught her breath.

"Ward — what —?"

"Nothing of great account," he said quickly. "And don't bother Jeff about it."

To this she paid no heed at all, catching her husband's eyes and beckoning vigorously.

Jefferson Chesbro was a stocky, slightly balding man, with a round, pleasant face and shrewd, steady eyes. At forty he was an even ten years older than Sebastian. His smile and the pressure of his hand, told of his feelings.

"Good to see you, Ward! What's the word?"

It was Helen Chesbro who answered. "His arm, Jeff."

Chesbro's smile became a frown of quick concern. "What happened to it?"

"Later," Sebastian soothed. "You get back and wait on trade, else there'll be no profits."

"Profits be damned! What happend to you?"

"Well, if you must know, Sam Lester and I met a mite of trouble out at Sheet Iron. Somebody tried a couple of shots. They nipped me slightly and did for one of the mules, which hurts a lot more than this scratch on the arm."

Jeff Chesbro's frown of concern deepened, but before he could press the matter further, his wife took command.

"No more questions just now, Jeff. This arm needs caring for. Ward, you come along. Your eyes are cloudy, and that could be fever. Don't argue!"

Gathering up rifle and coat, Sebastian indicated the saddlebags with a nod.

"Best put these out of sight, Jeff. Right on a thousand in specie in them. Homer Shadworth sent it over from Fort Bidwell by Bill Wiggin. He'll take all the flour and other staples you can get through to him. The military are holding a lot of wagon folks in Surprise Valley and won't let them cross the mountains for fear they'll get into the area of operations and complicate things. They're dependent on Shadworth for flour and he's running short. I can, of course. But I won't have a pack string free for another two weeks, at least."

Jeff Chesbro pursed his lips, considering. "I'll do all I can, of course. But I won't have a pack string free for another two weeks, at least."

"Figured that might be," Sebastian said, "So I brought my full string, and I'll put your stuff on most of them, going back. Bill Wiggin can take it on from my place."

Turning to follow Helen Chesbro, he again met the eyes of the girl in the cloak. And he knew, by the now open and inquiring interest in them that she'd been listening and had missed nothing. As the interval of their locked glances lengthened she colored slightly and looked away, showing a stiffening of her head and shoulders.

Sebastian's lips pulled in the faintest of smiles. Likely, he decided, she was fresh from the Presidio at San Francisco, come along with some officer relative of the Regulars. At any rate, almost a sure bet to be of the Army, and not forgetting it for one haughty minute, either.

When a man stepped through the door at the end of the counter, he moved far away from the wet and bitter world outside. Here was a cozy living room, touched with comfort and simple charm. Beyond ran a short hall, with doors opening off either side of it, and the far end leading into a warm, brightly lighted kitchen.

Here a coffeepot steamed and savory odors lifted. On a table, half a dozen freshly baked loaves of bread gave

40

off their cooling fragrance. Along with the drag of fatigue, a touch of fever, and with raw hunger an insistent, hours-old demand within him, the impact of all this made things a little unsteady for Ward Sebastian. He stacked his rifle in a corner, hung his coat and belt gun on a wall peg, then dropped into a chair, his words running low and husky.

"When I was a kid, my idea of an angel was a fat, pink and white infant, perched on a cloud. Now I know better. A real angel is a woman like Helen Chesbro, in a kitchen like this. If I could just have a cup of that coffee —!"

Smiling mistily, she poured it for him, and his sound right arm and hand trembled as he lifted the cup and drank eagerly, draining it of its hot goodness. He sighed deeply.

"Now — now I live again!"

With deft, swiftly snicking scissors, Helen Chesbro cut away the sleeve of his shirt and the bandanna that had served as a bandage. After which it was necessary to soak the cloth free of the wound. Fully exposed, this showed as a shallow, but now inflamed slash across the heavy muscles of the upper arm.

He had a jaw-clenching moment of it when the hot water first made contact with the open wound. But presently it became a soothing comfort which drew the fever from him, along with the throbbing pressure that had begun to build up in the arm. Cooling balsam oil, with its clean, pungent fragrance was smeared over the wound, followed by a snug bandage. In contrast to the raw misery he'd ridden with down across the long miles

41

from Sheet Iron, Sebastian now knew a vast and relaxing ease. He looked up at Helen Chesbro.

"The angel image," he said, "becomes increasingly real."

She laughed softly and gave him a gentle buffet alongside the head.

"Bosh! You should save that kind of talk for Anne Biglow. She was by today, wondering when you'd be in town again."

"Checking up on me, eh?" he drawled, dryly humorous.

"Of course. What with all the Indian trouble and frightful rumors flying, and you in the middle of it all, is it any wonder she worries? Ward, that girl is lonely. Don't leave her so, too long."

"Harley Ritter still ambitious, you think?"

"Exactly. Very ambitious. And insistent. Anne's father has taken him into his law office as a partner. The idea of further partnership between a Biglow and a Ritter could be catching."

"You got a point, there," Sebastian admitted. "But Anne can quit being lonely the minute she says the word. All she has to do is marry me, come out to the ranch and set up housekeeping. I've told her that."

"All of which isn't the easiest choice in the world for a girl like Anne to make."

"Why not? It's the same choice every wife since the beginning of time has had to make."

"Yes, and no. You have to consider the time and the way things are, Ward. A ranch, isolated and lonely, way out there toward Tule Lake. No neighbor within miles.

42

Almost in the center of this Indian trouble. I think I'd have to love a man very deeply, to follow him to that ranch."

"Now I say — bosh!" stated Sebastian flatly. "I know you better than that. You'd follow your man to such a ranch, or through hell with your shoes off, for that matter. Anne's big trouble is that she's always had a very settled life, and she wants all things laid out to that safe, secure pattern. But you just can't schedule a whole lifetime that way; you got to live it as you go along. Anne is going to have to understand that, and accept it."

Helen Chesbro eyed him in her gentle, comtemplative way.

"You're an unruly, restless scoundrel, Ward Sebastian. The woman who finally domesticates you will be a wonder."

His grin showed. "Sam Lester says the one great chore in any man's life is to keep some designing woman from earing him down and putting him in an easy chair."

"Sam Lester! That tobacco-eating old pirate!" She sniffed scornfully. "Do you want your supper now or would you rather clean up and get into dry clothes, first?"

"I'll clean up."

One of the side doors off the hall led to a room reserved for Sebastian's use while in town. In here he achieved the final physical lift of a shave, a good wash and a change into clean, dry clothes. When he returned to the kitchen, Helen Chesbro showed a frowning irritation.

"This," she said, "is stark cruelty to a man half starved, as I know you are. But Jeff wants you out front, Ward. Do you mind too much?"

"Not if it's necessary. What's it about?"

"I don't know. But Jeff's upset over something."

"Knowing the man," Sebastian said, "he wouldn't be so without good reason. I'll go along."

CHAPTER
FOUR

Jeff Chesbro was talking with considerable vehemence to the officer who accompanied the girl in the cloak. As Sebastian came up, Jeff turned, plainly more than half angry.

"Sorry to drag you away from rest and food, Ward, but Captain Dillon here was insistent that he see you. Meet him. And — Miss Ashland."

The officer's handshake was brief, perfunctory, leaving the impression that it was purely a mechanical, not a natural courtesy. Giving him no better than he sent, Sebastian looked past him at the girl.

"My privilege, Miss Ashland. I know a Major Ashland. The last time I saw him he was on station at Fort Klamath."

"My uncle," she said.

Her glance was as always, clear and direct, but there was uneasiness in her just now.

"Captain Dillon," Jeff Chesbro said, "brings a somewhat unusual request, Ward. Demand is even a better word. I've explained that with all my pack outfits scattered somewhere between here and Crescent City, over on the coast, I can't possibly meet his demand right now. Also, I've done my best to convince the

45

captain you have important and definite use for your string. But —!" Jeff hunched his shoulders, turned up his hands.

Sebastian eyed the officer. "What about my pack string?"

Captain Judson Dillon was thin-faced, darkly handsome, with coal-black eyes holding the hard shine of an authority weighty to the border line of arrogance. The set of his lips was severe, and he carried himself stiffly erect. He spoke curtly.

"I am faced with the necessity of putting through a transport detail to Tule Lake in the shortest possible time. This automatically rules out wagons in favor of a pack train. I have some service animals available, but not enough to handle the detail properly. How many mules, Mister Sebastian, are you prepared to furnish me?"

While Dillon spoke, Sebastian regarded him intently. Here was a thorough-going military martinet, one with little patience or regard for anything civilian. Sebastian's reply was bluntly crisp.

"None at all! I can't do you a bit of good."

Captain Judson Dillon came up slightly on his toes.

"Perhaps you did not understand me, Mister Sebastian. I did not ask, *would you?* I asked, *how many?*"

Now it was Sebastian's eyes which took on a hard gleam.

"I told you — *none!*"

A taut silence fell, broken by the rustling of Connie Ashland's cloak as she stirred restlessly. She was a fairly tall girl, full of a mental and physical vigor which made

46

it impossible for her to be a negative quantity. Now, as she watched the clash of wills between these two men blaze and grow, a deepening concern held her.

Captain Dillon spoke again, his tone flat, almost metallic.

"You brought a pack string into Yreka this evening, Mister Sebastian?"

He had a way of emphasizing the "Mister" which was an irritant in itself. Sebastian swung his shoulders and tried to hold on to his rising temper.

"I did."

"How many animals in the string?"

"Twenty-five. No, make that an even two dozen. I lost one along the trail."

"I'll settle for two dozen. I'll take them."

"Take them! Mister, what are you talking about?"

"Just what I said. I'll take them."

"You're forgetting something," Sebastian said harshly, rough anger beginning to spill out of him. "That string of pack animals happens to belong to me. Strictly private property!"

"Which," Dillon retorted, "in the name of military necessity, I have full right and power to commandeer. Which is a step, if you force it so, I'm fully prepared to take."

Ward Sebastian had another good look at this man, his eyes darkening.

"Captain, that would be a damned high-handed piece of business. I would not recommend that you try it."

Dillon shrugged. "We'll see."

Sebastian turned to Chesbro. "Jeff, can this fellow be serious?"

Chesbro nodded. "Afraid so. And he can do it."

Sebastian came slowly around to face Dillon again. "When would you be wanting the mules?"

"I expect to leave for Tule Lake not later than noon, tomorrow."

"That's making it mighty rough on the animals. They should have at least one full day of rest before going out again. And when they do go, they should be carrying food supplies to a lot of civilian folks spread out across a big slice of country. Plenty of women and kids among these, too. But maybe, Captain, you just don't give a damn if they go hungry?"

Captain Judson Dillon flushed, his face tightening at the bite of truculent sarcasm in Sebastian's words.

"I'm well aware of civilian needs. In my judgment, however, the present military need is greater. So, that is the way it will be."

Jeff Chesbro spoke up. "Ward will be recompensed for the use of his mules?"

"Certainly," Dillon said. "The government will pay a fair rental per animal, per day."

"And of course I'll be going along," Sebastian said.

Jeff Chesbro came around fast. "Not with that arm of yours, Ward. That wouldn't be smart."

Sebastian shrugged. "The arm will have to do. When this chore is done with, I want my mules back in decent shape, not saddle-galled by careless saddling and packing or broken down from overloading."

"The Army," Dillon said stiffly, "has thoroughly capable packers. We don't need —,"

"The Army," cut in Sebastian, "has blundered in this matter. Somebody didn't count right. And I'm being forced to pay the difference. So, Sam Lester and I will be going along to handle our own string!"

Twin spots of red showed in the swarthiness of Dillon's narrow cheeks, and his black eyes went as hard and shiny as bottle glass. Plainly, this man despised any other will than his own. But finally he nodded.

"Very well. You understand, of course, that while the use of your pack animals will be paid for, you will be on your own time and at your own expense and risk."

"Still worth it," Sebastian said curtly. "Where do I load?"

"At the supply depot in the warehouse at the eastern end of this street."

"Good enough. I'll be there at daylight. Have your stuff ready. When I travel, I like an early start."

"You will not start until I say so," Dillon said, "for you will be transporting military supplies, and so require an escort."

Temper that had begun to smooth out a little, now flared anew, and again that edge of roughness spilled out of Sebastian.

"Captain, I'm willing to meet you half way. But I'll not stand for any deliberate pushing around. I know the trail between here and Tule Lake like I know the back of my hand. I know how much of it can be covered in an average day's travel. I know what the weather was coming in today and what it will probably be tomorrow.

I'm leaving early so that I can reach Mike Golway's ranch before full dark, and spread my blankets under cover. If you want to pull out late, and put in tomorrow night in a wet, cold camp, that's your business. But don't try and hold me to such a deal, because I won't stand for it!"

Under the whip of Sebastian's words, Captain Judson Dillon drew himself up ramrod-straight. Plainly he was furious. But he knew he'd been reminded of the practical limits of his authority. He turned abruptly away, his words flat and toneless.

"Very well. In the morning, then. Shall we go, Connie?"

The girl followed him out, her head high. She had her final glance at Sebastian, and her eyes were bright with anger. Jeff Chesbro let out a long breath.

"Man, you really took the spurs to him! You think it wise?"

Sebastian shrugged.

"I've seen considerable of the military, Jeff. I've found there are two kinds of officers. The right kind and the Captain Dillons. I like the right kind, but don't like the Captain Dillons. Now I'm heading for the kitchen, where I'll eat until Helen throws me out."

The best part of an hour later, replete and at ease, Ward Sebastian leaned back in his chair and began packing his pipe. Across the table from him, Jeff Chesbro spoke what was uppermost in his mind.

50

"All right. You got your ribs well padded with grub. Now let's have all the story about that Sheet Iron business."

Sebastian told it.

Chesbro frowned. "Wouldn't Sheet Iron Butte be pretty far west for any of Captain Jack's Modocs to be operating just now?"

"Too far," nodded Sebastian, cuddling a match over his pipe bowl.

"Yet," hazarded Chesbro, "there's always the chance some young buck, anxious to prove his manhood, might have been skulking."

"If I could be sure such was the answer, I'd feel better about the affair," Sebastian said slowly. "The Modoc and his purposes I can figure pretty well, for I know what forces are pushing him around. It's the white renegade I wonder about."

"Would you be suggesting Provo Holt or some of his?"

"Maybe," Sebastian admitted. "Holt and Yance McCloud were at Orcutt's corral when Sam Lester and I pulled in, so it couldn't have been either of them. But it might have been Jake Ruby."

Helen Chesbro came over and pulled up a chair. She braced her elbows on the table top, cupped her chin in her hands and studied Sebastian with that grave and penetrating wisdom.

"You brought something back with you this trip that you never did before, Ward. It is in your eyes — a sort of shadow. And not because of what happened at Sheet Iron, either."

Sebastian tipped his head and met her glance.

"Shrewd lady," he said gravely. "I know you won't be satisfied with less than all the story. But I warn you, it is not pretty. You heard about the peace palaver at Natural Bridge?"

"Some," Jeff Chesbro said. But the town is full of rumors and you don't know what to believe."

"Well," said Sebastian, "nothing peaceful came out of the meeting. It broke up in another ruckus."

"What started it?"

"Same old story, apparently. The olive branch was offered, but strictly on the white man's terms, backed by the eye of a gun looking down the Modoc throat. Under such conditions, the answer was foregone."

"So," said Jeff Chesbro grimly, "it now begins all over again."

"Always, it seems, there is cause for worry," Helen Chesbro put in.

Sebastian's sober glance touched her again. "More than worry for some, Helen. After the row at Natural Bridge, the Modocs split up. From all the signs, Captain Jack brought most of his people down the west side of the lake to the lava-bed stronghold. They bothered no one along the way. But about a dozen others, led by Scarface Charley and Hooker Jim, cut down the east side of the lake. And they left a lot of blood and tears behind them."

Helen Chesbro caught her breath. "The Laird ranch is over on the east side. Angus, Mary — Lorna —"

The regret in Sebastian's tone turned it very gentle.

"No more, Helen. Mrs. Laird and Lorna are all right. But Angus and Obe Adams —!" He shrugged.

Helen Chesbro went slowly white.

"Ward, you're sure?"

"Very. There were others. George Roblett and his two boys. Also, Pete Thurman and Nick Dutra. I told you it wasn't a pretty story."

Helen Chesbro straightened in her chair, flaming.

"The fiends! The cruel, bloody handed murderers! Always before I knew a certain sympathy for the Modoc. But no longer." Tears welled up in this gentle woman's eyes, quenching the blaze of outrage there, and her voice softened to little more than a whisper. "Mary Laird, and Lorna — and those other women! Those poor souls. What a terrible thing!"

"All of that," Sebastian nodded. "I've lived one day I'd just as soon forget, but know I never will. The worst was in getting some of the womenfolk away from, well — what had been their men."

"The fiends!" choked Helen Chesbro again. "Those filthy, murdering Modoc beasts!"

"No," Sebastian said. "Not that, Helen. When you say such things, you're only thinking once. But when you think again, then you take it back."

"Ward Sebastian, you're not defending —?"

"No, not defending. Nor blindly blaming, either," he told her soberly. "For it's always been so easy to blame the Indian for everything. I'm not condoning the raid, understand. Anything but! Yet, neither am I forgetting all the treacheries and other dirty affairs we whites have been guilty of. Much that the Indian has done, we've

53

driven him to. And in many cases have been fully as savage."

"But those poor women," she protested. "Their world shattered, all their dreams and hopes just — just ashes."

"I know. The women always take a mean beating in this sort of business. That goes for the Modoc squaw, too. If you'd ever heard the squaws, as I have, wailing their dead, then, as Sam Lester says, you'd realize that tears are a pretty common possession."

"Of course, Ward, of course! Only, why do things like this have to happen?"

He considered for a moment. "We'll know that, perhaps, when we find the answer to human greed." He pushed back his chair. "Well, there's a couple of people I got to see." A fleeting smile leavened the soberness in him. "I can hear Sam Lester howl now when I tell him about tomorrow."

Jeff Chesbro stirred restlessly.

"I don't feel too good about that, myself. I don't like to think of you taking a wounded arm out on the trail. Couldn't Sam Lester do all right by himself? He could keep an eye on things."

Sebastian flexed his arm carefully. It was stiff and sore, but definitely better since Helen Chesbro's ministrations. The ominous throb of fever had left.

"It'll heal just as well along the trail as it would if I laid around in town, fretting and worrying over my mules. Besides, I don't dare let Sam go alone, else he'd be liable to set out to lick the whole United States

54

Army, single-handed." He chuckled. "For some reason, Sam and the military just don't get along."

"Time like this makes me realize there's a lot of unbalance in the world," said Jeff Chesbro. "If it wasn't for men like you and Sam and Bill Wiggin covering the rough trails between here and Surprise Valley, and the men handling my own pack outfits to Crescent City and back, I'd be out of business, and quick! You fellows take all the hardships and the risks, while I sit here warm and dry and safe, benefiting by your misery."

The humor continued to grow in Sebastian's face, warming and clearing it. He got to his feet and slapped Chesbro on the shoulder.

"My good friend, don't ever feel sorry for me. You're the one who deserves sympathy. Cooped up inside, arguing with bargain hunters, trying to keep track of what you got and what you need; adding up figures and more figures, worrying over bills to collect and bills to pay.

"Me, and others like me? Well, say the weather does come up a little mean at this time of the year and on through winter. But think of spring and summer and early fall, when all the world's a garden and we're right out in the middle of it, listening to the orioles singing in the buttonwillows, and watching our shadows go dancing down the trail ahead of us. No, sir, Jeff, don't you ever go to feeling sorry for the likes of me. I'm doing all right by myself!"

CHAPTER
FIVE

It stood toward the upper end of Oregon Street, a two-storied, gabled house, surrounded by a split-picket fence. Several of its windows glowed warm with light, and a high stone chimney let out scented pinewood smoke to swirl and flee across the wet, dark sky before the drive of a bustling wind.

The girl who opened the door to Ward Sebastian's knock, and who stood lined against the light of a short hallway, was small and graciously made. Her hair framed her head with a smooth sleekness, and her face held a clear perfection of feature. She caught her breath, exclaiming: "Ward!"

"A thick night to be calling, Anne," he said, closing the door behind him. "But sight of you makes it more than worth while."

He took off his hat, slid out of his coat, then reached for her and pulled her close.

"Come here, girl," he said a little huskily. "There are times when the trails can be mighty long and lonely." He drew her up and found her lips.

For a moment she seemed responsive. Then all the small perfection of her became full of a taut resistance,

56

and with her hands spread against his chest, she forced herself away, protesting breathlessly.

"Ward! Please! There's a time — and a place —!"

"What's wrong with this time and place?" He stared down at her and a shade of harshness crept into his tone. "Why shouldn't I kiss you, right here and right now? Anne, when are you going to get rid of this damned touch-me-not pose?"

She answered him out of a small, shaky confusion.

"It — it's not a pose, Ward. But you — you don't give me time to think. You come in out of the night, almost like a part of it with all its wildness and roughness, and the chill of its wetness on your face. You — you overpower me. Which frightens me. And I don't like to be frightened."

Again he studied her, and a quietness of manner settled on him.

"Sure," he said. "I understand. Sorry!"

As though sensing withdrawal on his part and fearful of it, she caught at his arm, hugged it, brushed a cheek against his sleeves.

"I'm so awfully glad to see you, Ward — truly I am, for I've worried. And been lonesome. It means so much to have you here!" She clung to his arm a little tighter. "Come in by the fire."

The hallway led into a fairly spacious parlor, and here a wide hearth was filled with the ruddy welcome of rippling flames. At the far end of the room a door let into a small study, where the drone of a man's voice sounded. Sebastian's glance was questioning.

"Dad and Harley Ritter are going over some sort of law brief," Anne Biglow explained. "Come say hello."

As a man, Milo Biglow was full of a spare, gray, almost austere dignity, part naturally come by through the background of an old and honored family, part acquired over the years of his profession. As a lawyer he was highly regarded, and there was some talk that he might be offered a position of responsibility with the government in Washington.

Just now he sat in a big chair before a flat-topped desk, his head back, his eyes half closed, his slender hands steepled, as he listened to Harley Ritter's reading of the law brief. As Sebastian and Anne entered, Ritter broke off and got to his feet.

Milo Biglow stirred slightly in his chair, then spoke without turning his head.

"Who is it?"

"It's Ward, Dad," Anne said. "Ward Sebastian."

"Indeed! Well — well!" Biglow rose from his chair and turned. "It has been some time, Ward."

"Almost two months, sir." Sebastian shook hands, then turned to Ritter. "Harley, how are you?"

"Good enough," answered Ritter. "You might say — lucky. For Mr. Biglow has taken me into his office as a junior partner." He said it with some smugness, as though gloating over an advantage gained.

Sebastian eyed him briefly. "So I heard. Congratulations! Ever the busy little bee, eh, Harley?"

There was a cut of sardonic irony in this which brought a quick, slightly frowning glance from Anne

Biglow, and added more color to Harley Ritter's full and already florid cheeks.

Ritter was of average height and inclined to fleshiness. There was a soft, pink, well-fed look about him; a neat man, always clean-shaven and smelling faintly of bay rum. A man made for comfort in a comfortable world. His mouth was small, his lips full and red. He smiled easily and often; too easily and too often, some men felt. Ward Sebastian was one of these.

"How has it been with you, Ward?" Milo Biglow asked.

"The usual, sir. A ranch to keep an eye on, and a lot of pack-trail miles to ride. It all adds up to work."

"Plus a considerable element of danger, I imagine, what with all this Indian trouble going on. And just what are we going to do with that Kentipoos, that Captain Jack and his confounded Modoc followers?"

"By the present look of things, just about exterminate them, I'm afraid, sir."

"Which is the sensible thing to do," put in Harley Ritter. "And the quicker it is done, the better for all."

Sebastian regarded him intently.

"You really mean that, don't you, Harley? You'd condemn those people to death without fair trial or recourse. Is that the kind of law you practice and believe in?"

Harley Ritter stiffened. "It's the only realistic solution and you know it. America has a destiny to fulfill, and can't afford to let any bunch of savages hinder her march toward it."

A faint, mirthless smile touched Sebastian's lips.

"Ah, yes, destiny! Harley, would you be going noble on us and quoting Benton?"

"Perhaps. If so, what's wrong about it?"

"That could depend on where you stand," Sebastian said. "Personally, I consider it one of the mealy-mouthed utterances of all time. Manifest destiny! Real high sounding off the tongue. But when Benton voiced that statement he worded a hypocritical justification of armed conquest and robbery that will one day tie the conscience of America in knots."

Milo Biglow lifted a mildly admonishing hand.

"Now, now, Ward! I don't like to hear you speak that way. Thomas Hart Benton was a great man who spoke with wisdom and prophecy."

"I admit the prophecy, sir, but question the wisdom," Sebastian said dryly. "As a nation we've marched across a continent. But for the most part on the somewhat questionable basis of might making right. Senator Benton may have phrased it another way, but that is what it really amounts to — the right of might."

Milo Biglow's shoulders straightened and a faint flush crept up his gray cheeks. He spoke with some stiffness, as though his professional integrity had somehow come under fire.

"I have every legitimate sympathy for the Indian's unfortunate lot. I believe I've the right to say that no one has championed the rights of all men more sincerely than I."

Ward Sebastian tipped a lean head. "I'm sure of that, sir." He turned to Anne. "These men have work to do. We should leave them to it."

60

"Just a minute," said Harley Ritter. "There is some word around town that a Modoc raid of ranches along the east side of Tule Lake massacred a number of whites. What have you to say to that?"

"Simply that it's true," Sebastian answered quietly. "I know, because I was there. I helped bury the victims. It was a grim business, and pretty hard to take, emotionally. Yet, logically reasoned, it must be charged up as one of the costs of war, and when has war ever been anything but a sad and bitter business? The victims of the raid were all male. No woman was harmed in any way."

"Well now," exclaimed Harley Ritter sarcastically, "that was damned considerate of the noble red man, wasn't it?"

"In the light of certain past events, you might even call it so. Be very convenient, don't you think, Harley, if we whites could somehow forget the Ben Wright affair?"

"Twenty years ago," scoffed Ritter. "A long time. And I've heard the story told all to Ben Wright's credit."

"So have I," Sebastian retorted. "But also I've heard the opposite from men like Henry Gallatin and Frank Searchly. With me, their word is beyond question. Oh, there's no doubt that Mister Ben Wright and his crowd did a most thorough job of cold-blooded murder that day."

"Twenty years ago," repeated Harley Ritter. "All you have to go on is hearsay. You weren't there to see."

"Nor," pointed out Sebastian curtly, "were you. It happens, however, that I have seen some evidence of white savagery. At Horse Creek, and at Desolation Flat. There wasn't a single young and able-bodied warrior at Desolation Flat; just squaws and children and old men. So, when Provo Holt and Jake Ruby and others of their stripe finished there, they certainly left behind the white man's curse. You see, Harley, there appears to be a double standard which I just can't subscribe to. When a Modoc kills, in defense of his ancestral homeland, he's a blood-thirsty savage. But when the white man kills, in the process of robbing the Modoc of his homeland, then he is merely fulfilling what he likes to call a manifest destiny. My friend, who is the hypocrite?"

There was a combative glint in Sebastian's eyes, and the color in Ritter's well-barbered cheeks again grown deeper. Milo Biglow lifted a protesting hand.

"Enough! Both of you! You're on an issue which only the historians may find answer to. I suggest you leave it to them."

"So do I!" declared Anne. "Ward, you come along with me!" She tugged at his arm.

To Milo Biglow, Sebastian said, "Sorry, sir." Then he let Anne lead him back into the parlor. She faced him at the hearth and dug into him with some asperity.

"Did you have to act so?"

"How?"

"You know what I mean, arguing the way you did. And when Harley told you of going into the office with Dad, you — well —!"

"I congratulated him, didn't I?"

"Yes — sarcastically. Was that necessary?"

He pondered this, scrubbing his chin between thumb and forefinger. The hint of a smile pulled at his lips.

"I must have figured so."

"But, why?"

In Milo Biglow's study the drone of Harley Ritter's reading had begun again. Sebastian crossed over and closed the door, his smile widening as he came back to the hearth.

"Will that have old Harley jumping! He'll be imagining all sorts of things, now. And — where were we, anyhow? Oh, yes, why did I spur Ritter, even gently? Well, quite frankly, Anne, I don't like friend Harley. He gets under my skin."

"Why should he? He's never done you any real harm."

"He does every time he steals even a little bit of your favor. I could fry him alive for that."

She stamped a small foot. "Please! This is serious. What's the true reason you don't like Harley?"

Sebastian considered for a time, then spoke slowly.

"It is because he represents a type I don't care for. The soft, calculating, safe-and-sure type, who can argue loudly that extermination of Captain Jack and all his Modoc people is necessary and just, but who would faint dead away if forced to come face to face with them out in the lavas. The kind that never know a truly generous thought for someone less fortunate. The kind who like to decide the fate of men with words, but never deeds. These they leave to a hardier breed."

"Harley isn't that way at all," she protested. "How can you say such things?"

"You asked me," he reminded.

She looked up at him. He loomed lean and tall, dark-faced with a deep weathering burned and beaten into him by sun and storm. In the reserved depths of his eyes lay the reflection of far distances, often looked at and fully understood. This man belonged completely to the open country.

As always, he stirred her. Even now, while exasperation and a degree of anger held her, he stirred her. She faltered.

"Just — just when I'm sure I could cheerfully beat you, Ward Sebastian, then I — well —"

He laughed softly, caught her slenderness in the circle of his sound right arm.

"Better, much better. Suppose we forget all about Harley Ritter and talk just about us. When are you going to marry me and come out to the ranch like a good and dutiful wife?"

Again he drew her up, found her lips. Again for a little moment she answered his ardor and his cup was full and sweet. Then the soft submission of her became that taut resistance, and when he let her go she moved swiftly apart from him and stood staring at the fire, her breath running rapidly, her cheeks flagged with color. She spoke in a small, contained murmur, as though meant only for herself, but which, in her agitation, was loud enough for him to hear.

"I mustn't be carried away! I must think on this — think!"

64

"Think?" Sebastian's tone carried a faint edge. "How much thinking do you need to do, Anne? You should know your own mind by now."

She did not look at him, avoiding his eyes.

"You don't understand, Ward. This isn't a casual sort of thing. It is such a — well — such a final decision. So it is necessary that I consider carefully, that I know my full mind."

"And you don't, is that it?"

"I don't know whether I know or —"

His laugh was curt. "Now there is a perfect example of feminine reasoning, perfectly expressed."

She came around to face him, flaring. "It's not funny at all! You've no idea what you're asking me to do."

"I know exactly what I'm asking you to do. Just — just that you marry me. It's as simple as that." His tone gentled. "There isn't a thing to be afraid of, Anne. I'll cherish you very dearly."

She blinked back a small start of moisture in her eyes.

"I know — I know! It isn't that, Ward. While you frighten me a little at times, I know you never mean to. No, it isn't that. It's what you would take me away from, what you would take me to. It — it's that ranch —!"

"What's wrong with the ranch?" he defended. "It's a good ranch. Some day it will be a great ranch. Just now the headquarters isn't too big, but plenty big enough for the small likes of you. It's well built and comfortable. You'd be warm and safe and —"

"Safe? In a country where people are being massacred right and left? Ward, that's it — that's entirely and fully it. I just couldn't stand being there alone, with you away so much, running that pack train of yours all over creation. No, I just couldn't stand it!"

"But you wouldn't be alone, Anne. Bob Gayle and his wife never leave the place. Mrs. Gayle would mother you to death. I tell you, there isn't a thing to worry about."

"Yes, there is," she half whispered. "Loneliness, on that ranch —" She turned to stare into the fire again.

Sebastian marked the unconscious grace of her turned head, the small perfection of her every move and pause. He thought of what he had said to Helen Chesbro earlier in the evening; how if a woman loved a man the way she should, she'd follow him wherever the need of his life's work took him, knowing he would care for her and guard her faithfully.

Apparently, he decided bleakly, that sort of thinking was just pale pipe smoke, the thinnest kind of mistaken male theory.

Abruptly he was thoroughly weary. He turned toward the hall.

"I have to hit the trail again at daylight tomorrow, Anne," he said across his shoulder. "So I've got to get some sleep."

She followed him to the hall, worried, reluctant, uncertain.

"You see," she said. "You see how it is? You've been with me such a little time, and already you must leave. It's the trail again. It would always be the trail. Married to you, a woman would feel she was married to a shadow. Oh, Ward, isn't there some other, better way? Couldn't there be a business of some sort, here in town?"

"No," he told her quietly. "No, there isn't any better way. To be any damned good in this world, a man must follow his own star, not one that someone else selects for him. And a woman must follow her man. Ward Sebastian, as you see him now, is one person. Ward Sebastian, tied down in town to some job or business that he hated, would be someone else entirely. You wouldn't care for him and he wouldn't care for himself."

He got into his coat stiffly, favoring his left arm, lips tightening at the drag of his coat sleeve across the bandaged wound.

Anne did not notice. She was staring straight ahead, seeing things of which she was fearful; wanting life, yet afraid of it. At the moment there was a strange, pinched look about her, stealing the beauty from her.

Sebastian started to reach for her, then halted the move. For should he find any sweetness of response, it was almost sure to be immediately overcome and soured by the inevitable resistance, by that recoiling caution. And the result would be poor flavor indeed, to linger on the lips of a lonely man. Better by far the free kiss of the rain. He donned his hat and opened the door.

"Good night, Anne," he said.

The rain was there, waiting for him, wet and chill and clean. The wind pushed it at him, pushed it past him. A gust of it reached Anne Biglow, challenging her. She gasped and backed away from the challenge, closing the door quickly.

A chill, dark sky pressed close to the earth and wept upon it drearily. Dawn light was a gray and dismal phantom, peering cautiously across the rain-slimed roofs of Yreka town. At the east end of Miner Street, men and pack mules were grouped before the military supply depot. Troopers, sour in mood because of the early hour and the weather discomfort, worked sullenly by lantern light.

Supplies brought forth were loaded on the pack mules, with Ward Sebastian and Sam Lester supervising this activity closely. Crusty old Sam was openly caustic in his opinions, and once, after argument with a couple of surly troopers over the arrangement of a pack, he turned to Sebastian, fuming.

"Now it's a mighty good thing you and me are handling our own string, Ward. These here johnnies got no idea how to load a critter for this kind of country."

One by one the packs were made up, tarpaulins spread, hitches thrown. Sebastian was content to leave most of this to Sam, finding that his left arm could stand considerable favoring. On waking in the cold, predawn darkness, the wounded member had been locked in painful stiffness. By the time he'd dressed, things had loosened up a bit, but he accepted philosophically the fact that a certain amount of pain and physical misery was to be his companion down all the long miles and hours of the day ahead.

Just as they finished with the final animal of the string, Captain Judson Dillon appeared, moving into the ragged area of lantern light. Morning's dank touch silvered his long overcoat with a beaded wetness, and his thin, dark cheeks were drawn and set by its chill. He was not alone. With him were Provo Holt and Yance McCloud.

Soundly surprised at this, Sebastian managed to hide his feelings behind an impassive mask. He nodded to Dillon.

"I'm ready to pull out, Captain. Where's that escort?"

Dillon's manner was stiff, his answer curt.

"It will be here. You'll wait for it. There's considerable loading to be done yet, including Mister Holt's string. We'll all travel together under the eye of the same escort."

"Captain," protested Sebastian quickly, "that wasn't last night's agreement."

"Agreement? There was no agreement," Dillon rapped. "You said you would leave at daylight. I said you would leave when I gave the word, not before. Any other impression you may have is pure assumption on your part, Mister."

Provo Holt, watching and listening, showed a sardonic smile. He was a lithe, smooth-featured man, fair of hair and with pale, cold eyes. Behind the mocking gleam of his glance as it rested on Ward Sebastian lay the naked flame of an unrelenting hatred. Now, in the words and manner of Captain Dillon, Holt read discomfiture for this man he hated so, and he was quick to enjoy it.

Yance McCloud, lank and dark-faced, hid whatever he felt behind a surly indifference, real or assumed. His lips were still swollen from last night's contact with Sebastian's fist.

Sebastian centered all his attention on Dillon.

"Captain," he said bluntly, "it won't do. Last evening I told you I would travel at daylight. You conceded the point. I've kept my word and I expect you to keep yours. Sam, bring up our horses! We're leaving."

In the reflected lantern light, Dillon's black eyes showed a glitter.

"If you persist, Sebastian, you'll force me to take measures."

It was in Sebastian to fence around a point just so long. The morning's bleakness was in him, along with a certain physical seediness because of his arm. His patience and temper were short. Now, of a sudden, he was coldly, wickedly angry.

"Measures! What kind of measures! Take them and be damned to you! I suggest, Captain, that you climb down off those precious shoulder tabs of yours. They may be all of life and the keys to the gates of heaven to you, but to me they don't mean a damned thing. See that you don't start something you can't stop. Because I'm prepared to ride this thing through, right up to the top, Captain. Where the big brass lives. Then we'll see what they think of this kind of deal. It could be you'll end up minus some of your shine!"

This fiery defiance held Captain Dillon silent for a moment, and in this stillness Provo Holt spoke, mocking, sardonic.

"Big talk, Sebastian, big talk!"

Sebastian whirled on him.

"Who asked you in on this, you Goddammed squaw killer?"

From the murky half dark behind Sebastian, Sam Lester spoke with a gently finality.

"That's it, Ward. Tell 'em! Wherever it leads, I'm with you!"

The tone of hard-flung words, almost as much as their content, striking across the bitter dawn, alerted men and drew them in. Troopers began gathering at the edge of the thinning lantern glow, their breathing a hard sibilance against the sudden, frightened silence.

Under the whip of Sebastian's caustic words, Provo Holt had gone very still, his face draining of color. His lips made a pinched line across his teeth, and when he spoke, his words barely seeped through, husky and toneless.

"Sebastian, I've had just about enough of that from you. If you didn't have Lester backing your hand —!"

"I can take care of that, too," said Sebastian swiftly. "Sam, you stay out of this completely. Mr. Holt, here, is going proud on us. It'll be interesting to see if he's as good with a gun on me as he was on that poor little frightened squaw at Desolation Flat. All right, Holt! You want it, start it! I've been waiting a long time for you to get up nerve enough to make the try. Go ahead, damn you!"

As he spoke, Sebastian stripped open his coat, flung it back, so that the gun at his hip was ready to his hand. Now he waited, putting the weight of further decision on Provo Holt.

Violence, or the promise of it, was an integral part of any soldier's life. This Captain Judson Dillon knew and understood full well. But that violence, when it came, to a degree was an ordered violence, planned and maneuvered, and made legitimate under the title of war.

Here, however, was something else. This was more than a mere wrangling of words and the clash of wills. This was naked, deadly challenge, deliberately thrown. This was a violence leaping raw and savage out of the dark depths of a pit of hatred between two men, and holding to no law but that of the fang. It was something that had to be stopped before turning into the rip and roll of gunfire, and men dying on the sodden earth.

Captain Dillon also realized that he was faced with a deadlock that could be broken only by someone making concession, and though making concession at any time — especially to a civilian — was gall and wormwood to him, he made it now. He stepped between Sebastian and Holt and spoke sharply.

"Enough of that! Whatever your private quarrel, you'll not go through with it here. Mister Sebastian, if you insist on traveling without escort, you'll be held completely responsible for every ounce of supplies in those packs. If you are prepared to accept that responsibility, you may pull out immediately."

72

Sebastian was hearing Captain Dillon's words, but he was watching Provo Holt with a narrow, bleak alertness, trigger-sharp for any hostile move Holt might make. He saw and measured the rioting rage in the man. But he saw something else, too, which was the thin shine that suddenly glistened on Holt's face when Captain Dillon intervened. This, also, he recognized for what it was. In spite of the frigid dawn, that shine was of sweat, the sweat of relief.

Sebastian's lips curled. He buttoned his coat again and nodded.

"Very well, Captain. Have no worry about the supplies. They'll be well taken care of. All right, Sam!"

They climbed into their wet saddles and got the reluctant pack string into motion. They filed past the outskirts of town and on down the run of the valley, keeping well to the eastern edge of it, and so avoiding any further entanglement with the military host that filled this lowering dawn with wood smoke from grudging, low-winking camp-fires, and gave off an over-all rumble that was an accumulation of a thousand smaller sounds.

It was, thought Sebastian, like the growl of some great, insensate beast, bound on the blind purpose of destruction. He knew clear relief when, with Sam Lester leading, the pack string made a curving swing into the Tule Lake trail, and the valley and all it contained, was left behind.

Now the way was almost directly east, and the rain, whipping in from an angle just a little south of east, slanted its raw chill against Sebastian's face. He tipped his head into the drive of it and called up the stoic patience and mental detachment a man had to achieve if he were to endure the inevitable punishment of the slow miles and hours, with all the physical trials that went with them.

There was a trick to it. You retreated far inside yourself, clinging close to the warm fire of living that lay there. Your outer self became a tough rind of resistance, against which wet and chill might beat fruitlessly, and which only the wearing acid of fatigue might finally soften. You placed your thoughts, so far as you could, on the better moments of your life and kept them there, while handling horse and mules of the string instinctively.

So the hours passed and the miles, and because these things were fixed and real, when the pack string had put enough of each behind, then you again came even with the surly, dark lava mass that was Sheet Iron Butte. Here Sebastian's thoughts jerked abruptly from that locked inner corner of himself and turned hard and wary.

Up ahead, Sam Lester likewise rode high and alert and watchful, his head swinging as he carefully studied the butte and the rain-misted sweep of country all round about. But today there was no threat, no harm in any of it.

The pack string moved steadily across the sagebrush flat in front of the butte, and on to the rain-furrowed gulch that led to the higher ground where the junipers and mahoganies massed in dark, gray-green wetness. Only once did the mules break the even cadence of their progress, and that was to drift a little wide of the spot where lay the carcass of their unfortunate fellow that had died yesterday.

Here Sebastian's horse also showed a small measure of unease, swinging aside, snorting and tossing its head as it passed. Sebastian saw that the coyotes had been working on the carcass during the night, opening the paunch, so now it lay sodden and shrunken, looking as though it had been dead for days instead of merely hours.

Within a short week, he mused grimly, there would be only the bones left, marking another spot of minor violence beside a lonely trail.

CHAPTER
SIX

The Golway Ranch lay at the eastern end of the Chinquapin Meadows. Strategically placed as a stopover spot on the trail between Yreka and Linkville and the Tule Lake country, Mike Golway had built shrewdly to meet the needs of such a stop. There were corrals to contain saddle and pack animals, and sheds in which to feed and shelter them. There were two long bunkhouses and a sprawling ranch house to do as much for humans.

Mike Golway himself was a great, shaggy bear of a man who could be as rough and ready as any occasion demanded, or as openly gentle. His wife was a strapping, black-eyed Warm Creek Indian squaw, displaying something not far from real beauty in an olive-cheeked, Junoesque sort of way. The ranch helpers, inside and out, were members of the same peaceful tribe.

Here, at day's end, a freezing dusk pinched remorselessly down across the meadows. But inside the ranch house a roaring fire filled the wide, deep hearth and, stripped to his shirt sleeves, Ward Sebastian stood before the flames, turning slowly from side to side, welcoming the heat that soaked into him and drove out the bone-deep chill of long hours in the saddle.

Even closer to the heat, like a gaunt old dog, Sam Lester hunkered on his heels, his gnarled, rope- and rein-calloused hands spread to the fire, his bony features cut into sharp bronze by the flickering light. Mike Golway came in with a strong three-fingers of whisky for each of them. Sam put his drink away with a single avid gulp, then sighed deeply.

"Mike, you understand the needs of a man. You surely do!"

Saying which, Sam pushed to his feet and turned to Sebastian.

"Be done with your drink, boy; then get that shirt off. I want to look at your arm."

Sebastian flexed it. "It feels pretty good. It's all right."

"So you say. But there's been a seediness in you all day, and I could tell, when we were unpacking, that the arm was troubling you. So, we look at it, and no argument. Mike, I'll need some hot water, some balsam oil if you've got it, and clean cloth for a bandage."

Mike Golway was immediately curious. "What's wrong with the arm?"

Sam briefly sketched the incident. Mike exclaimed gustily.

"Seems they've pushed Captain Jack and his people past all reason — driven them to skulking the trails and taking shots at whoever passes. Only last night it was Jake Ruby who put up with me, and he with a bad leg. He'd been sniped at."

Sebastian came around.

"Jake Ruby, Mike? With a bullet wound?"

"That's right. He's not a man I greatly care for, him having been in on that Desolation Flat slaughter." Turning to leave the room, Mike added: "It's been a rule of mine not to deny shelter to any man, red or white, but in this case I was thinkin' that justice would have been served if that Modoc bullet had gone through Jake Ruby's head instead of grazin' his leg."

Mike went out and Sebastian turned to meet the gleam in Sam Lester's eyes.

"So-o!" murmured Sam. "Mister Jake Ruby! Well, you said he stumbled at one of your shots."

Sebastian nodded, his face hardening. "Now we know. And as long as we're certain, we'll keep it to ourselves. Don't say any more about it to Mike."

Golway was shortly back. Sam put Sebastian on a stool before the hearth, stripped the shirt off him, removed the bandage and bared the wound. Mike Golway made critical observation.

"It doesn't look too bad," he decided. "Yet it is the sort of thing to drag a man down somewhat. Now it is lucky —"

He broke off, tipping his shaggy head as he listened. He went to the ranch-house door and opened it. The lamplight, pouring out, reflected on Army blue, all ashine with rain's wetness. A man spoke.

"Mr. Golway, I am Lieutenant Philip Ashland. I have with me my sister, a guide and a detail of eight troopers. I hope you can find room for us."

78

"That I can, Lieutenant," boomed Mike with his big heartiness. "A lady with you, you say. Bring her in, man, bring her in! There's a bunkhouse your men can use."

The officer said, "Thank you, Mr. Golway. Go on in, Connie. I'll be with you as soon as I see to the men."

Then it was Mike Golway saying, with a touch of quaint, Old World courtesy, "Ma'am, you honor my house."

She stopped just inside the door, which Mike closed quickly behind her, shutting out dusk's fierce, unrelenting breath. Under a poncho of heavy canvas, she wore her long, blue cloak. The rain had thoroughly soaked the hood of this, so that now it lay wetly across her hair and framed her chilled face. She stared at the hearth with its ruddy, leaping flames and spoke in a taut, hushed tone.

"A fire — really! Warmth! It's hard to believe."

"Come right up to it, Ma'am," urged Mike Golway. "And you'll not be minding the bare back and shoulders of this man here, for he's a bit of a wound that needs care. Did I get the name right? It's — Miss Ashland?"

"Yes. Constance Ashland."

Acutely aware of his naked torso, Ward Sebastian had begun hurriedly donning his shirt. Connie Ashland spoke quickly.

"Don't be silly, Mr. Sebastian. Leave that shirt off until your arm is cared for, or I turn right around and go outside again."

Mike Golway exclaimed. "You know the man, Ma'am?"

She nodded. "I met him last night in Yreka. I thought then that he was a very stubborn person. I hope he is not going to act the same now, for I'd dearly love to move closer to that fire."

Sebastian met her direct glance, and far back in his eyes a glint of dry humor grew. He shrugged.

"You win, Miss Ashland."

She slipped out of poncho and cloak, hung them on a wall peg and stepped up to the hearth, slim hands extended. Again she spoke in that hushed way.

"For the first time in my life I can truly appreciate what fire has meant to mankind down through all the ages. Never have I been even half as cold!"

"Mean weather," Sebastian said. "I wonder why you should be out in it?"

She was quiet so long he thought she did not intend to answer. But finally she turned her head and met the inquiry in his eyes.

"You said you knew my uncle, Major Ashland. Well, when my brother Philip was detailed for duty up here, too, I just came along. I'm an Army brat, you see, so must follow the flag. For Philip and Uncle Ross are all I have."

Riding the long day out through the frigid rain had chilled her cheeks until they were like flawless marble, only now beginning to pick up a faint touch of color under the head of the fire. Her rain-dampened hair was tousled, and her face, relaxing and softening, took on some of the wistfulness of fatigue, which made her seem very young and appealing.

Gruff old Sam Lester, ill at ease because of the proximity of her, became all thumbs and left feet as he tried to work on Sebastian's arm. And when her glance touched him, Sam's efforts grew even clumsier. She smiled at him.

"Poor man. Let me."

Before Sebastian could object, she had taken over. As she examined the wound she pursed her lips disapprovingly.

"Men!" she exclaimed. "How ridiculous they can be! Especially stubborn men. Knowing such deep concern over the welfare of a mule or a horse, while taking all manner of foolish chances with themselves. As it happens, Mister Sebastian, this wound is in far better shape than you deserve. For which you owe great thanks to that very nice lady who took charge of you at the trading post in Yreka last night."

Mike Golway had gone to see about supper. Sam Lester, warmed inside and out by whisky and the fire, moved well away from the flames, leaving Sebastian and Connie Ashland somewhat alone. Of necessity she stood close to him. Her head was bent and she seemed to feel the intentness of his watching glance, for the color in her cheeks slowly deepened and a quickened breathing swelled her throat.

Sebastian thought of someone he'd been with for a little time last night. He tried to picture Anne Biglow in Connie Ashland's place at this moment, doing what she was doing, after a long day of real hardship. He found it a picture he just couldn't frame; it wouldn't come alive.

Under the spur of this disturbing realization, he frowned and stirred restlessly.

Connie Ashland looked up, spoke with a quick contriteness.

"I've been clumsy — I've hurt you?"

He shook his head. "Not in the slightest."

"But you flinched, and you're scowling."

He smiled at her concern. "Maybe it was just the thoughts of a stubborn man, spurring him."

"They must have been uncomfortable thoughts," she declared. "Probably the stubborn man was realizing he should have stayed in Yreka, knowing his precious mules would have been properly cared for, after all." She finished setting the bandage. "There, that is taken care of."

Sebastian reached for his shirt. "Miss Ashland, a stubborn man thanks you greatly."

Lieutenant Philip Ashland, men quartered and secure for the night, came into the ranch house out of a black world where the rain was thinning and the cold deepening. He shrugged out of his sodden overcoat, his glance reaching eagerly to the hearth and fire. He saw his sister sitting there, looking up at the tall, saddle-leaned man beside her, smiling over some remark that had been made. The young officer moved up beside his sister, dropped a hand on her shoulder.

The tall man turned, and recognition came to both he and Phil Ashland. Last evening, back in Shasta Valley, these two had mildly argued the rights of a

82

military camp set across a trail and a pack train traveling that trail.

"Lieutenant," the tall man said, "we meet again. I'm Sebastian, and yonder old catamount is Sam Lester."

"Philip Ashland, here. And my sister, Constance."

Ward Sebastian nodded. "Your sister and I met in Yreka last night."

"Oh, yes, of course. She was with Captain Dillon when he — you — well . . ."

Sebastian chuckled briefly. "Captain Dillon and I did argue some. But everything came out all right."

"Captain Dillon sent me ahead for two reasons," Phil Ashland said. "One was to get Connie under sound shelter for the night. The other was to come up with you and furnish escort the balance of the way. I hope that is agreeable with you?"

"Of course! In fact, I was led to believe there would be an escort, set to leave when I did, this morning. But there was none ready."

As though sensing a touch of censure or criticism of his superior officer somewhere in this, Phil Ashland spoke with some stiffness.

"Captain Dillon has his problems."

"I can understand that," nodded Sebastian dryly. "For that matter, these days we all do. Actually, I doubt there is any danger of a raid of any sort on a supply train between Yreka and Tule Lake. On the other side of the lake, yes. That is wide country out there and the military forces thin. On this side, however, just the opposite is true. I doubt that even the most reckless spirits in Captain Jack's band would be foolish enough to attempt a raid, hereabouts."

"I," said Connie Ashland, "just finished putting a dressing on a wounded arm. Yesterday evening, in the Chesbro store in Yreka, I overheard a little of the explanation of how and where you received the wound. Yet you say there is no danger along the trail between here and Yreka?"

"That," said Sebastian, "was not the result of any attempted raid. There was nothing to raid. The pack mules were traveling under empty saddles. That was just a private try at my scalp, for private reasons."

"I suppose it is none of my business by whom and for what reason?"

"It's a long story," he evaded, "and an unpleasant one. I doubt you'd enjoy it."

"Then it is none of my business!"

Mike Golway came in, his big voice rumbling.

"If you're hungry, now's the time!"

They ate in the kitchen of the place, a huge room, with a single long table running down the middle length of it, and warmed by a great stove standing in one corner. Golway's wife, and a younger Warm Creek squaw, hovered over the stove with its steaming pots and pans, and brought the food to the table, moving with soft padding feet and silent shyness. The food was plain, but it was clean and savory and plentiful.

The meal done, they went back into the other room, where Phil Ashland began getting into his overcoat. His sister exclaimed in protest.

"Phil, do you have to go out again?"

He nodded. "I've just had a good, hot meal. I want to see how my men are making out, cooking their own rations on that bunkhouse stove. I won't be long."

Sam Lester also reached for his coat. "Me," he said, "I'll be takin' a look at the mules, Ward. Then I'm turnin' in. Morning comes early to my old bones." He bobbed his grizzled head to Connie Ashland. "G'night, Ma'am. Get your beauty sleep. Not that you really need it, of course," he added hastily.

She smiled at him. "Good night, Sam."

Ward Sebastian had his pipe going, and he chuckled as the door closed behind old Sam.

"You've made a conquest, Miss Ashland. With most women, Sam finds it hard to even be polite."

"Why is that?" she asked.

"I can only guess. Perhaps something that happened to him a long time ago. A lot of men are scarred that way. Anyhow, from what I've been able to observe, the two things Sam seems to have the least use for in this world, are women and the military."

She seized the opening quickly.

"You're not exactly fond of the military yourself, are you?"

Sebastian sucked deep at his pipe and the smoke curled about his lean head.

"I wouldn't put it that way. Rather, say that like some other civilians in these parts, I resent the need of having the military about."

"While I," she retorted, "doubt the military is finding any great pleasure in being here. Certainly Captain Dillon and his men must be finding little to cheer about, having to make camp along the trail on a night like this."

Sebastian shrugged. "For that, Dillon's men can thank their captain's stiff neck. You may remember me arguing the point with him last night, insisting on an early start so I could reach this ranch. If Captain Dillon had been willing to accept the word of a civilian, he'd be sharing this comfortable fire with us."

She was watching him, studying him. His glance was fixed on the fire, his chin jutting slightly as his teeth clenched his pipe stem, and little knots of muscle bunched at his jaw corners. He was sober, frowning a little.

"You really are bitter at us, aren't you?"

"No." He shook his head. The military can't help being here. They're under orders. But they are a large part of the thing that is keeping this stretch of country in violence and bloodshed. They are the gun aimed at the head of the Modocs. Put it that the military is symbolic of what some people feel is unjust oppression. I happen to be one of these."

"You mean your sympathies are with the Indian and against your own people?"

He shook his head again.

"It's not that simple. Sometimes I almost wish I could be all one way or the other. A few days ago I helped bury several men I've known well, victims of a surprise raid by some of the wilder Modocs. It was rough business, even rougher trying to comfort the womenfolk of these men. These were people of my own kind of blood, and at the time I was very bitter, hating

86

all Modocs — all Indians. Later however, when I'd cooled off some and began totaling up everything — well . . ." He shrugged.

"Totaling up, what?"

"The Ben Wright affair. General Crook's remark at Northfork Canyon. Desolation Flat and other such occasions."

"I still don't understand."

Sebastian looked down at her. She was sitting bolt-upright, her shoulders squared, her chin tilted.

"Miss Ashland, you mean you've never heard of Ben Wright and his gallant crew?"

"No, I never did."

"I'll tell you, and let you define real savagery. There was to be a feast to celebrate a new-found peace between the white man and the Modoc. This was all the white man's suggestion, and he would furnish the food. Only, the food was to be charged with strychnine poison, and —"

"Oh, no — no!" exclaimed Connie Ashland, color draining from her cheeks. "Not such a thing as that! It couldn't have been . . ."

"Yet it was!" said Sebastian grimly. "As in all such things, there are claims and counterclaims. Yet it is a matter of record that one Ben Wright, leader of the whites, laid in a big supply of strychnine before leaving Yreka for the meeting with the Modocs. Also a matter of record is the final outcome of the meeting."

"You, you're trying to tell me," she said tightly, "that the Indians ate the poisoned food and — and —?"

"No. They didn't eat the food. The Modocs had gathered peacefully, once more believing in the word and good will of the white man. Yet, when the food was ready, there was something about it all that aroused the suspicion of the Modoc chief, and he ordered his people not to touch the food until the whites had begun to eat. Realizing that their fine scheme of wholesale poisoning had misfired, Wright and his crowd opened up on the Modocs without warning and shot them down like rabbits. Wright, himself, killed the father of Kentipoos, or Captain Jack as he is most commonly known."

Connie Ashland was biting her lips, her eyes big and dark with feeling. Her voice ran low.

"I find it awfully hard to believe that white men would even contemplate such a thing as that."

"Consider then, Crook's remark at Northfork Canyon. 'Nits,' he told his men, 'make lice.' The record shows that they took him at his word. When the killing was done with, there, left were only some half-dozen papooses that had been overlooked in the slaughter. There has since been much talk made over the kind care given these orphaned unfortunates by General Crook and his troopers. I wonder how much of that care was for show, how much for shame?"

"You — you damn us utterly, don't you?"

"No. And if I've upset you, I'm sorry. I just happen to feel strongly about these things. Perhaps it is the hypocrisy I can't stand. If the Modoc pulls a raid, it is a massacre. If the white man pulls a massacre, he calls it a surprise attack. In the past, Miss Ashland, a number of Modoc have worked for me on my ranch. Others have done the same for Frank Searchly and Henry Gallatin. We know them as human beings, not animals to be hunted down and exterminated."

Sebastian took a short turn up and down the room, then paused beside her again.

"It is virtual extermination they are facing now. Because this thing must be all the white man's way, and no other. Men curse Kentipoos, Captain Jack. Yet he never did want war with the whites. All he has ever asked for was a just peace for himself and his people. But rather than give him that just peace, the white man is set to exterminate him and all his kind. Which the Modoc now understands beyond all doubt, and is why he is forted up in the lavas, ready for a final showdown."

There was a stir of movement at the door of the room. It was the young Warm Creek squaw who had helped Golway's wife at supper. Now she was bringing some hefty chunks of wood to the fire. She moved quietly, her face expressionless but for the glint of a shy excitement and interest in her black eyes as she darted a swift glance at Connie Ashland. She knelt at the hearth, placed the wood expertly, then rose and left as quietly as she had entered.

Connie Ashland looked up at Ward Sebastian, frowning.

"Just like a beast of burden, and you let it be so. You didn't offer to help her. Is that the real measure of your sympathy for the Indian?"

Sebastian met the frown with a faint smile.

"I thought you would speak of that. As it happens, the real reason I didn't help her, was out of regard for her feelings. Had I offered to handle that wood, it would have shamed her terribly; made her feel she was unable to serve, and so was unworthy. It is the Indian way. Incidentally, would you regard her as a savage, something to be exterminated? Well, she is of the Warm Creek tribe, an offshoot of the Modocs, but without their fierce, bitter pride."

The girl beside him was still for a long time. Finally she stirred and sighed deeply.

"You have given me much to think about, Mr. Sebastian."

His pipe had gone out. He tapped the dottle from it, packed it afresh and lighted it. Through the curling smoke he watched her.

She had settled back once more, relaxed weariness again touching her features with that soft, composed wistfulness. Her eyes were drowsily half-lidded, and their lashes lay curled against the smooth curve of her cheeks. The beauty in her, Sebastian decided, was that of spirit and boundless health, of youth's gay and eager interests, and with enough of maturity's seasoning to add a full, warm womanliness.

Her head began to nod, dropping lower. Sebastian went to the inner door and called Mike Golway. When Golway came in, Sebastian pointed.

"There's a young lady about to fall asleep, Mike. How about getting your wife in here to take over?"

"This blessed minute!" cried Mike.

Connie Ashland straightened in her chair, flushing warmly as she met Sebastian's amused glance.

"My manners are terrible," she said. "But I was a pig at supper, and now this wonderful fire." She yawned, tapping her lips with the back of her hand.

"Get a good night's sleep," Sebastian advised. "It will be another long day tomorrow, and we start early. You see, on that point I'm still a stubborn man."

Golway's wife showed at the inner door, the younger squaw peeping from behind her. Mike's wife looked at Connie Ashland and spoke just two softly guttural words.

"You come."

The girl hesitated.

"Go along," Sebastian said gently. "They'll care for you like they would an infant. Good night!"

At the doorway she paused looking back at him.

"Good night!" she echoed.

Sebastian turned to the fire again, reluctant to leave it for his blankets out in one of the bunkhouses. His thoughts were all on the girl who had just left the room. Hardly more than twenty-four hours ago he had laid eyes on her for the first time. But she left him just now with the feeling that he had known her a very long time indeed. A consciousness of her presence still held in the room.

The outer door opened and Lieutenant Philip Ashland bustled eagerly in.

"Wicked cold out there," he said, pushing close to the hearth. "Where's Connie?"

"Being put to bed by Mike Golway's womenfolks. She was falling asleep in front of this fire."

"Rough on her, a trip like this," said the young officer soberly. "I should have made her stay in Yreka. For that matter, I did try and discourage her coming along. But she was determined, dead set on going through to Fort Klamath. Got a mind of her own, Connie has. Feels if she's not around to look after me, I'll get in all sorts of trouble." He laughed deprecatingly. "I'm only four years older than she, yet that still leaves me a younger brother in her eyes."

"Lieutenant," Sebastian said, "you have a very remarkable sister. I'm happy to promise you that tomorrow night she'll again rest in comfort and under sound shelter."

"At your ranch?"

"That's right."

"Your place is close to the actual trouble area?"

"Close enough to be near, far enough away to be safe."

"We leave early?"

"Right! It is always good trail wisdom to make an early start. So, we'd best turn in ourselves."

Donning coat and hat, Sebastian stepped out into a black and freezing world, and along with Phil Ashland hurried to the bunkhouse.

There would, he knew, be ice along the trail in the morning.

CHAPTER
SEVEN

It was a freak morning, one of those rare interludes wherein a reluctantly departing fall season mustered enough vitality to hold back, for a few hours at least, the remorseless, onrushing advance of winter. As Ward Sebastian had surmised, ice glazed every small spread of water beside the trail. But the sky had cleared during the night and when a couple of hours gone from Mike Golway's place, the pack train and its escort moved into the eye of a late-rising and faintly warming sun.

Past experience told Sebastian this was a weather condition of short duration, probably not lasting the day. Yet, while it endured, it made for a degree of cheer, and both man and beast reacted to it. The mules seemed to step out with a little extra spirit and the troopers of the detail shed much of the dourness they'd brought with them last night.

On all sides the world lay clear to the eye. West and north ran the distant bulk of the Siskiyous, snow massed at the summits, dark with timber below. East and south, beyond the flats, it was a rugged, broken world, studded with lava-darkened ridges and buttes, slashed with long running rims; empty, lonely, wild. Yet, over all there ruled a presence. South it towered. The mountain. The lofty, serene, pure pyramid that was Shasta!

Before sunup it had been an almost shadow thing, dim and ice-blue and cold, seemingly remote to a distance that was dreamlike. But the disclosing sunlight now brought it close and sharp in all its shining, soaring magnificence.

Connie Ashland couldn't take her eyes off it. She exclaimed to her brother as she rode with him for a time. After which she reined over beside Ward Sebastian to exclaim further.

"It just doesn't seem real," she marveled. "It is so pure and flawless in every way. It could be the mother of all creation, in a robe of spotless ermine. I think I could look at it forever and never tire!"

She turned in her saddle to look again. Her lips were slightly parted, her cheeks glowing, her eyes all ashine. She was, Sebastian saw, completely at home in that saddle, handling her mount with certainty and ease. An Army brat, she'd called herself. In which case, he decided, the Army had done a first-class job in raising and training her. He smiled at her exuberance.

"That mountain is pretty much the hub of our physical world here," he said. "When I was a boy, a very, very old and very wise Indian told me that once you lived close to Shasta and fell under its spell, then, no matter where else you journeyed, you must come back to the mountain again to find your happiness. There are times when I think the old cuss and his legend might be more than half right."

94

She considered this for a moment or two, her eyes fixed on the mountain. She nodded.

"I like the thought, anyhow."

She rode at Sebastian's side for a considerable distance. She inquired about his arm and he spoke truthfully when he told her it was much better. She became all eyes and ears and interest for the world around her. She asked about, and he identified the cedar, the mahogany and the juniper, the aspen and the choke cherry. A marmot, late in seeking hibernation, whistled defiantly from the broken lava fragments of an ancient rim, and she had to know the what and why of that too. When a mule deer, startled from a mahogany clump, went away in long, lunging leaps, she cried her quick delight.

She watched a hawk's far soaring. And when, from a great height, the clarion call of wild geese came down, her eyes shone with pleasure. So many things did she notice and ask about, Sebastian teased her gravely.

"The military should detail you as a scout, Miss Ashland. You don't miss a thing."

"This," she retorted simply, "is a new world to me. And I want to see it all; mountain, sky, birds, beasties — everything."

Ward Sebastian had been over this trail many times before. But never had it been as pleasant a journey as now, with this vivid, eager girl riding beside him.

Again, as last night, his thoughts went back to Yreka, to Anne Biglow, and in his mind's eye he tried to create an image of Anne in the saddle beside him, eager and interested in this world of his, as was Connie Ashland.

And again it was no use. The picture wouldn't come to life.

A shade of grayness crept into his mood. In these thoughts lay a growing uncertainty, and uncertainty he did not care for. A man made his own world, his own trail so far as he could; he did not wander, but traveled in a straight line. He liked to feel that he knew his own mind at all times. But now, about Anne Biglow, he was not sure. He kept trying to tell himself that he was, but the small, gnawing doubt was there, and it turned him moody.

As Sebastian feared, the brightness of the morning did not last very long. Well before midday a scud of overcast began to build up, squeezing the last drop of cheer from the sun, then blanketing it out completely. The world turned cold and mists lifted from the wet earth to layer all the flats and choke the gulches in dankness and a gray chill.

Connie Ashland reined a trifle closer to Sebastian.

"Now," she said, her tone subdued, "I grow a little fearful of this wild land of yours. The benevolence I saw in it a while ago seems to have entirely left, and in its place I sense a threat, a latent cruelty. It — it is a savage land, isn't it?"

"To the degree that makes it vital, yes, you might call it so," he agreed. "But it is a land of many faces. Wait until you see it in the spring. Then you'll forget all about such days as this one."

"I won't be here in the spring. As soon as this Modoc trouble is cleared up, brother Phil expects to be ordered to either a Dakota or Arizona Territory post. And I'll be going with him, of course."

"If," said Sebastian, "your leaving here depends on an end of the Modoc trouble, you'll still be around next spring."

She glanced at him, startled.

"You must be mistaken. Jud Dillon says that thirty or forty days at the outside will see the end of all resistance."

"Not a chance," Sebastian told her bluntly. "Captain Dillon and a number of other military minds are due for a surprise, an unpleasant one. They've simply no idea what they are going up against, and they refuse to listen to some of us who do."

The swift upswing of her head and stiffening of her shoulders forewarned argument.

"Would you claim greater knowledge of military problems than that of men trained in such things?"

"In a case of this sort, I would. I know the country. Captain Dillon, for example, does not. I doubt he has the slightest idea of what the lava beds are like. Where Captain Jack and his people are holing up is one of the most rugged, savage parts of the lavas. Any military tactics Captain Dillon and others like him have learned or studied in the past, simply won't apply. I'm afraid a lot of men will die before some minds wake up to the realities."

"But" she protested, "there aren't very many Modocs. Philip says our forces far outnumber them."

"Quite true. At least twenty to one. But the lavas cut such odds way down. Fighting in them, a Modoc warrior who knows them is equal to twenty white men who don't."

"You are a very positive man, aren't you, Ward Sebastian?"

He shrugged. "I never try and fool myself about facts, if that is what you mean."

They drifted into silence and presently Connie Ashland reined away to ride again with her brother and his troopers.

As Sebastian had prophesied the evening before, there was no slightest hint of trouble along the trail. They met no one, they saw no one. They moved through a world empty but for themselves; a world that steadily turned more gray and misty as the miles and the hours passed. Shasta became a pale and distant ghost, losing all substance until gradually there was nothing left. As the pack string progressed, the mists opened reluctantly to let it through, then closed quickly in again. The immediate visible area on all sides became one of a scant few hundred yards.

Bringing up at the drag alone, Ward Sebastian figured the passage of time and distance and made his estimate of time of arrival. The pace of the string had begun to slow, the mules showing the effect of the grind. Humans were feeling it, too; Connie Ashland's slim shoulders were beginning to droop. When, presently, Lieutenant Ashland chanced to turn his head, Sebastian beckoned him.

"The mules are beginning to wear down, Lieutenant, and it is going to be well after dark before we reach headquarters. But if you want to split your detail, we can send your sister ahead with Sam Lester to guide, and she can be under shelter and resting considerably before we get in."

"Thanks," nodded Phil Ashland. "I'll ask her."

Watching, Sebastian saw by the negation in her strong head shake that she'd have none of it. A little later she reined over to his side once more.

"So you are not only a positive man, but a considerate one. I thank you, but must decline your kind suggestion."

"Why?"

"Because I wish to."

A flicker of amusement showed in Sebastian's eyes. "And last night I was the one called stubborn! You intend to fight it out along this line if it takes all night, is that it?"

She gave him a ghost of a smile in return. "Exactly, my uniform-hating friend."

"Here — here!" he exclaimed. "I can't be that bad."

"Well, almost," she insisted. "You've certainly made it plain that, by and large, your opinion of the military is anything but complimentary."

"Not so," he protested. "I think —"

"It's quite all right," she cut in. "I've been doing some thinking and I've arrived at the conclusion that we in the military can stand a little jostling and criticism — that it is good for us. We live in such a tight little world of our own, we are apt to lose our perspective. Your kind of rugged independence and straight thinking is good for us."

"Then," Sebastian said, "you're not entirely out of patience with me?"

She was silent while a faint flush built up in her cheeks. Presently she asked, "Did I act so?"

"A little, I thought."

"A little, I was."

"But not now?"

"No, not now. However, I'm not promising a thing. At any time I may change my mind and claw you furiously."

"That," he declared, "is a gamble I'm happy to take. I wish home was closer than it is. You're growing pretty weary, aren't you?"

"A little," she admitted. "But perhaps the miles would be shorter if you used some of them to tell me about yourself. I've already confessed that, like all military women, I follow the flag. But what about you? What is your life?"

He got out his pipe, packed and lighted it, and the keen, clean tang of tobacco smoke curled back across his shoulder as he rode.

"Only what this kind of country has to offer," he said. "I came into it by wagon train as a small boy. My father left me the beginnings of a ranch. I've managed to build that up pretty well, and to get this outfit of pack mules together. Between the two, I make a pretty fair living."

"And what is the rest?"

"That's all of it. That's my life."

"You make it sound entirely too simple. It actually must be very rugged."

He shrugged. "There are plenty of softer ways of earning a living, I suppose. But I like my way. I move around a lot. I see the country. I live with the seasons and watch them change. I'm my own boss. It's a good life, and a free one."

And that, thought Connie Ashland, was the vital part of it all for this man — this Ward Sebastian: that he answer to no other authority than his own; that he have independence, complete and unquestioned; that he be free — free in the widest sense of the word.

Riding in silence, she mused on this, contrasting it with her own situation. As far back as she could remember, her world had been a succession of military posts, first with her uncle, then with her brother Phil, after he had won his commission. In many ways it had not been at all a bad life, but also, when she considered it honestly, neither had it been a particularly rewarding one.

Boiled down to the bare bones of fact, the dominant note had been one of monotony, of a changeless sameness. For, no matter where the military post, nor how large or small, basically they were all alike, run to the same set of rules and regulations, governing utterly the lives of its members, either by outright command and authority, or by almost equally confining military tradition.

It was a life which, baldly put, in all too many cases skidded dangerously close to being one of genteel poverty. You had to make the best of quarters often decrepit and hardly livable. You owned few worthwhile possessions because the constant shifting around discouraged the acquiring of such. You became one of a little group and to that group you clung desperately, because if you moved outside it you ran into contrasts which taunted you and which you often secretly envied.

So, you followed the flag and left your youth and beauty somewhere along that trail of regulation and monotony. You knew a degree of economic security, but also a sense of frustrating economic limitation. You became faded and, without realizing it, perhaps a little dowdy. Because the system and its regulations had done so much of your thinking for you, had ruled you and made you its own creature.

And because of the confinement of your thinking and your movement and associations, you lost contact with the wider civilian world, and you would never be able to fully regain it. So, if you lived to retirement, you ended your days on a lonely fringe, engrossed in your pension and, for what they might be worth, your faded memories.

Connie Ashland knew a stir of unease. Was such, she wondered, the sum total of all that lay ahead of Phil and herself? Was that the full worth of their youth, with its vigor and ambitions and its dreams?

Several times in the past she had done some casual thinking along these lines, but never had she reached so deeply, or dredged up so many truths to look at. It had taken the presence of this tall, hard-jawed, fiercely independent and self-reliant man to bring her to such a searching analysis of the present and the future. And as she considered the picture, the unease in her deepened.

102

Daylight ran out and night came down and the pack string plodded heavily on through full dark. Chill and weariness dragged at the riders, made them silent and withdrawn. Sebastian knew full sympathy for the girl riding beside him, but he also knew it would not help in any way to offer it. So he thought ahead to a spot in the trail where he would be able to lift her spirits.

The time and place came finally. Unseen on either hand in night's complete blackness, low lava ridges pinched in to make a narrow and a shallow pass. Sebastian knew the feel of the place, recognized the small echoes of passage which bounced back from the low rims. He broke the silence that had held between the girl and himself.

"Count twenty, slow, and then look. You'll see the lights of home."

Startled from a near stupor of physical exhaustion, Connie Ashland did as he suggested. Halfway through the count, she felt her horse swing left a trifle, then, reaching full count, she saw the lights he said she would.

Home! She whispered the word to herself, and all the depths of its meaning flooded her and brought the hint of a sob to catch at her throat.

On Ward Sebastian's part, he was standing high in his stirrups, studying those lights. For there were a number more than there should have been, and some were flickering and uneven. Up at point of the string, Sam Lester held the mules back and sent his thin yell knifing across the dark.

"Get up here, Ward! We're runnin' into something. More military, I think."

"I'll go," called Lieutenant Phil Ashland. "I'll handle this." He was gone with a rush before Sebastian could answer.

They waited out the slow minutes, wondering. Across the black distance came the small emphasis of a sentry's challenge, followed by the faint echoing of other voices. Then Phil Ashland came spurring back.

"Troops," he reported briefly. "A company of the 21st Infantry and one of Oregon militia. Quartered at your ranch, Mr. Sebastian, until further notice."

They went ahead, and the flickering lights resolved into campfires, and there were sentries and gruff voices everywhere, so it seemed to Connie Ashland. Buildings loomed abruptly to block the way and the ammoniac odors of wet corrals lifted sharp and cold.

Phil Ashland moved up beside Sebastian. "If you'll just see that Connie is made welcome —?"

"Of course," Sebastian said. "First thing."

He helped her from her saddle and guided her stiffened steps to a ranch-house door, which, when he pushed it open, let out a flood of light and warmth. In the room beyond, white-haired Mrs. Gayle and black-haired Kitty Dutra were talking to a grizzled major of Infantry. Mrs. Gayle exclaimed:

"Ward! You made a fast trip. We weren't expecting you for days, yet."

"Military business," he told her briefly. "And here is another guest for you to take under your warm wing.

104

Miss Connie Ashland. She's had a long, rough day of it, Mother Gayle. So if you . . ."

"Connie Ashland!" It was the grizzled officer exclaiming in deep, rumbling tones. "Good Lord! Don't tell me it's that niece of mine! Not my Connie?"

"But it is," Connie cried. "It is, Uncle Ross!"

Then she was past Sebastian and in Major Ross Ashland's arms, laughing a little, crying a little.

"Bless my soul!" rumbled the major. "Bless my calloused soul! My own Connie — all grown up into a young lady."

He held her off and looked at her fondly, grinning from behind a somewhat ragged mustache.

"Yes, sir, a young lady. And a damned handsome one, too. Child, what brings you way out here? I thought you safe and secure at the Presidio. Why didn't you stay there?"

"With both you and Phil on duty at Fort Klamath? Indeed not! Where my menfolks are, that's where I will always be."

"Humph!" growled Major Ashland. "So Phil's been ordered up here, too? Well, it doesn't surprise me. They're bringing them in from all over. I must get out and see the boy."

With Connie inside the circle of his left arm, Major Ashland held out his free hand.

"Glad to see you again, Sebastian. And sorry to clutter up your premises with my men and myself. But the Gallatin and Searchly ranches are already overrun with troops, and I'm here under orders from Colonel Wheaton."

Ward Sebastian had known this bluff, hardy, down-to-earth officer for some time, and liked him. Now, as he shook hands, he said:

"Quite all right, Major. Seems there is a common problem to face."

"Problem is the right word," said the major, his lips pulling ruefully. "I only hope the top command has some understanding of how big the problem really is."

Kitty Dutra was standing quietly, watching and listening, dark eyes intent on Connie Ashland. Now Sebastian turned to her.

"Kitty, meet Miss Ashland. Connie," and the word came unconsciously to his tongue, "this is Mrs. Dutra. Between her and Mother Gayle, I know you'll be made comfortable. And now, Major, I've a string of pack mules to look after."

"Of course," said the major, "and I'll be wanting to see Phil."

Connie Ashland looked at Sebastian. "My valise is tied to the saddle of one of Phil's troopers. If I could have it —?"

"I'll see that it is brought right over," he promised.

Out in the night, Major Ashland took hold of Sebastian's arm and spoke with some concern.

"You understand, of course, that I'm more than happy to see that niece of mine. But what am I going to do with her? I can't send her on to Fort Klamath, for, even if I'm lucky enough to escape a Modoc bullet, I won't be going back to Klamath for at least six months, perhaps not then. I doubt Phil will get that far, either, until this affair is cleaned up. So, Klamath won't do where Connie is concerned. I understand that Henry Gallatin and Frank Searchly have sent their womenfolk up to Linkville. Maybe we'll send Connie there, or back to Yreka. I'll talk it over with Phil."

Sebastian smiled in the dark.

"From what I've seen of your niece, Major, shipping her off by herself anywhere will take considerable doing. I suggest you quit worrying about her. She's welcome to stay right here at this ranch as long as she wishes. She'll have the company of her own sex in Mrs. Gayle and Mrs. Dutra. Later, if you and she and Phil work out some other satisfactory plan, good enough. Until then, consider everything settled."

"My friend," Major Ashland said, obviously relieved, "that's very decent of you. Puts us all in your debt."

"Not at all, Major. Just the other way round. Mother Gayle will rejoice. She's been much alone out here, and having your niece to fuss over, will make her happy."

"That Mrs. Dutra?" inquired the major. "Who is she? Mighty fine-looking woman, if I may say so."

"That Modoc raid down the east side of the lake widowed her," Sebastian explained. "She was living in an isolated spot, and obviously couldn't stay there alone. So I brought her here until the future straightened out for her. I've known Kitty a long time. She's had anything but an easy road of it."

"These frontier women of ours!" exclaimed the major. "I marvel at them. The way they stand up to the clubbings of tragedy and misfortune! You wonder where they get their courage."

107

Sebastian was silent for a stride or two, then spoke thoughtfully.

"Perhaps it is more than simple courage. It could be a special brand of faith."

CHAPTER
EIGHT

Connie Ashland awakened to a stir of movement, to the crackle of open flames, and to the good scent of fat pinewood smoke. Deep in a nest of blankets, she was snug and warm and so completely drenched with drowsy comfort as to be reluctant to move so much as a finger or a toe. With the lift of increasing wakefulness, however, came a growing curiosity, so she pushed up on one elbow to observe her surroundings.

In the gray morning light she saw a room of fair size, with an open hearth centering one wall between two tiers of well-stocked bookshelves. Another wall contained a window and a set of huge mule-deer antlers mounted on a shield of dark wood. A third wall lifted blank above the bunk she lay in, and beyond the foot of the bunk a low-topped bureau beneath a small mirror held a white china pitcher and basin. The fourth wall framed the door, and beside this was a rack of several guns. Plainly a man's room, comfortable, but with no frills.

Just straightening up after starting a fire on the hearth, was Kitty Dutra. She looked across at Connie and spoke pleasantly.

"Sorry if I woke you. I tried to be quiet. But I had to get this fire going, else you'd freeze, dressing. It's going to be another bitter day. You slept well?"

"Dreamlessly," Connie yawned. "I barely remember getting into bed. I'm afraid I was a nuisance to you and Mrs. Gayle, last night."

Kitty Dutra smiled. "Nothing of the kind. You did practically fall asleep during the hot bath we gave you, and again when you tried to eat supper. We decided then that you needed sleep more than you did food, so we hustled you off to bed. You're probably starved, now."

Connie was hungry enough and knew an eagerness to be up and about breakfast, yet at the same time was hesitant at leaving the warm comfort of the blankets. She used this moment of indecision to observe the room again.

"Whose?" she asked.

"Ward Sebastian's. And his father's before him. Now don't feel that you've run the man out of his bed, for you haven't. He rarely sleeps here, using the bunkhouse instead. He likes to keep the room about as it was when his father was alive. So, like now, it comes in very handy."

The hearth fire lifted and grew, crackling its ruddy cheer. A gust of warmth reached Connie and she pushed aside the blankets and moved swiftly closer to the welcome of the flames. She yawned again and let her night-shift slip from her, stepping from its crumpled folds. The firelight played rosily over her slim, supple beauty and Kitty Dutra, eying her, spoke quietly.

110

"My dear, you possess complete loveliness. See that you bestow it only on a man thoroughly worthy."

Before Connie, startled, could answer, Kitty Dutra slipped from the room.

There was warm water in the pitcher on the bureau. Connie washed and dressed swiftly for, even with the best the fire offered, some chill still clung to the room. Once she paused for a quick glance over the shelves of books. These, she saw, were solid books, plainly well-loved, for they were worn from much handling. On the narrow stone mantel above the hearth lay a couple of pipes, charred and blackened with use.

While brushing her hair, Connie thought of Kitty Dutra's remark and of the woman who uttered it. Had there been an edge of bitterness behind the words? And just what place did that black-haired, good-looking young woman have about this ranch house? She would, Connie decided, think more on the subject later, but right now an increasing awareness of hunger was uppermost in her mind. She sought the kitchen eagerly.

It was, she thought, a wonderful room, with a great stove creaking with heat and the air all aswirl with the enticing fragrance of warm food. Mrs. Gayle was there to greet her cheerily, and Kitty Dutra was busy over the stove. These two had already breakfasted, so Connie had the table to herself, and it wasn't until she had finished eating and was dawdling over a second cup of coffee that memory struck her and she started up guiltily.

"What a selfish creature I am!" she exclaimed. "So wrapped up in my own comfort, I completely forgot.

Mrs. Gayle, Ward — Mr. Sebastian — has a wounded arm!"

"I know," nodded Mrs. Gayle. "Sam Lester told me. Kitty and I cared for it last night. It's healing nicely."

Sounded the rumble of men's voices and a warning knock at the kitchen's outside door, and then Ward Sebastian and Lieutenant Philip Ashland came in, a weathered ruddiness beaten into their cheeks by morning's brittle chill.

Sebastian introduced the young officer to Mrs. Gayle and Kitty Dutra, then turned to Connie.

"And good morning to you, Miss Ashland. You're being well cared for?"

She looked at him with clear directness. "Much better than I deserve," she said simply. "I'm deeply ashamed of myself. Not until a moment ago did I remember your arm."

"No slightest reason why you should," he declared. "It's doing so well I've practically forgotten about it myself. Besides, right now the main concern is you. I'll let Phil explain."

Wondering, Connie turned to her brother. "What is it, Phil?"

"Why," said Phil, "it appears you'll be staying right here at this ranch for some time."

Connie was startled. "I don't understand. I thought Fort Klamath —?"

"That could be months away, Connie. Uncle Ross doesn't know when he'll be back there, if at all. And the latest headquarters order is that all troops in this immediate area will be held here until this Modoc affair is settled. So, I won't be going on to Klamath, either. Certainly you can't go there alone. Mr. Sebastian, being very generous, offers you the hospitality of his ranch. It would be much the simplest answer."

Connie shook her head quickly and with emphasis.

"We can't consider it, Phil. It would be a terrible imposition. I'll go on to Fort Klamath some way and make the best of it. But I absolutely refuse to . . ."

"No!" broke in Sebastian. "Don't use that word, it's too final."

"And meant to be," Connie said, a little stiffly. "I simply will not burden myself on people I scarcely know. It is not fair to them, or to me, either, for that matter."

"You don't understand," Sebastian argued. "This is a lonely land, where company is a rare luxury, and therefore valued highly. Besides, by agreeing to stay, you'll lift a lot of concern from the minds of your brother and your uncle."

She studied him intently, searching for the slightest hint of insincerity and finding none. Considering his last words, her instinctive opposition began to crumble. For, baldly put, she was an item of excess baggage for Phil and Uncle Ross to worry about. In all fairness she owed it to them to be of as little weight as possible.

Glimpsing her indecision, Sebastian went on.

"By your own admission, this is a different world than any you've known before. Well, here the word welcome really means what it says."

"You make it difficult for me to refuse," she admitted.

"Then don't think of it. We'll call the matter settled. If you've extra luggage in Yreka, Sam Lester and I will bring it through on our next trip."

"There is a trunk. At the Siskiyou House. It was to come up to Fort Klamath later by Army transport. It isn't a very large trunk."

"You'll have it," Sebastian promised. "Now, is there anything left in that coffeepot?" He turned to Phil Ashland, grinning, "Frankly, Lieutenant, I've tasted better coffee than that stuff your Army cook brewed this morning."

"Just as frankly," agreed the young officer, "so have I."

Kitty Dutra poured for them, and, when she handed Phil Ashland his cup, their eyes met in a quick, searching steadiness. Observing, Connie frowned slightly, for she wasn't too sure she approved of Kitty Dutra. She had to admit a dark beauty for Kitty, but there was also the capacity for a kind of slumbering intensity Connie did not understand, and was therefore wary of.

Finished with their coffee, Sebastian and Phil Ashland left, and Connie, moving to a kitchen window, watched them stride vigorously across the open interval between the ranch house and other buildings and the corrals beyond. She had always thought of Phil as being tall, yet Ward Sebastian beat him by an inch or two. In any event, they were a pair of fine, straight specimens, and Connie was startled to realize that some small part of her settled interest in one, now was being claimed by the other.

114

A trace of confusion over this fact caught her and she turned away from the window to find Kitty Dutra at her elbow, also watching the departure of the two men. Searching for a remark to cover her uncertainty, Connie said:

"Mr. Sebastian is a very considerate man, isn't he?"

Missing neither Connie's color or small confusion, Kitty Dutra smiled wisely.

"There never was a kinder. I've known Ward for years. He befriended my father and my brother beyond all reason, and now he is befriending me, allowing me the security of his home until I get my future unraveled a bit. You see, I recently lost my husband in a Modoc raid."

"Oh!" breathed Connie. "I, I'm sorry. I didn't know."

Kitty Dutra inclined her head slightly and made another of her startling statements.

"Even so I was luckier than some. I lost a husband. Other women, in the same raid, lost not only a husband, but all their future too. It wasn't that way with me, and there's a difference."

She became busy about the stove again, dark, silent, full of that contained intensity of feeling, leaving Connie to try to puzzle out the full meaning of her words. While pondering these, Connie turned again to the window.

The light of day had grown to fullness only slowly under the lead-colored sky. From this window, Connie Ashland looked out across a fairly level basinland, walled in the gray distance by low rims, beyond which, dim and shadowy with a misted remoteness, several buttes shouldered unevenly against the sky. Curving away to the north and east across the basin ran a road's vague outline.

Close in, around the corrals and outer ranch buildings, men in uniform moved. Horses and mules crowded the corrals, and a number of dun-colored Army wagons, with their bowed and swooping canvas tops, stood in line. In the clear open, past the corrals, campfires spread their layered smoke and a row of tents clung close to the earth. Where Connie stood was comforting warmth, but out there where she watched, the breath of both man and beast was a condensed vapor in the frigid air.

She saw noncommissioned officers moving among the troopers, directing them in various activities. She saw her uncle come out of a bunkhouse, speak with Ward Sebastian and her brother Phil for a little time, then turn back into the building. Beyond the farthermost limit of campfire and tent and corral, a sentry methodically stalked his post.

Abruptly, Connie Ashland knew fear. Not for herself, but for Phil and Uncle Ross and for those blue-clad troopers out there, for they were her kind, her people, a close part of the world she had always known. Here, however, was no drowsy Army post, where, except for routine calls and formations and drills to be stood or gone through, the days ran at languid tempo and held no threat at all. Here was but a short pause on the way to conflict, a final interlude before making rendezvous with that ominous something which lay waiting out there to the north and east where ran the vaguely outlined road.

Connie Ashland shivered as she turned away from the window.

Just short of midday, Captain Judson Dillon and an escort of sixteen cavalry troopers, led a long line of heavily loaded pack mules in at the Sebastian ranch. With them were Provo Holt and Yance McCloud. The mules were gaunt and slack-gaited under their packs and the men looked worn and punished and surly.

Standing at Ward Sebastian's elbow, watching the arrival, Sam Lester grinned like a wicked old wolf.

"Two night camps in open weather along the trail ain't sweetened them fellers any, boy. I wonder what that Cap'n Dillon thinks now of his judgment, alongside yours?"

"It doesn't matter," Sebastian said. "The land itself will teach him some facts — or kill him."

"That feller, Holt," said Sam, "he's got a hell of nerve, comin' in at this ranch."

"Some of the mules are his," Sebastian said. He added, a little grimly, "As soon as they are unloaded, he moves out!"

Captain Dillon had dismounted stiffly and briefly questioned a sergeant of the 21st. Now he came over past Ward Sebastian and Sam Lester. His eyes were sunken and bloodshot from lack of sleep, his narrow cheeks drawn and grubby with unshaven whiskers. He would have passed with a brusk nod, but Sebastian stopped him.

"A moment, Captain. The supplies I brought out from Yreka have been delivered to the care of Major Ross Ashland, who tells me further transport will be made by Army wagon. And, Captain, with your party is a man I don't care to have on my land. I refer to Provo Holt, of course. I'd appreciate it if you'd see that his animals are unpacked first, so that he can leave immediately."

"The man," said Captain Dillon, "happens to be traveling with me, strictly on Army business. Where I stop, he can stop. He has every right to food and rest and shelter."

"Not on my land or under my roof, Captain!"

Dillon looked Sebastian up and down. "Mister," he said, his voice harsh in his throat, "can't you do anything but try to obstruct Army affairs?"

"As it happens, Captain," Sebastian retorted, "I'm not trying to obstruct any Army affairs. This Provo Holt is no part of the Army. He's just a damned renegade, and whether he is under your authority or not, he doesn't stay one extra minute on my place. If necessary, I personally will run him off with a gun. If he turns on me, I'll kill him! Does that answer you, Captain?"

"I hope," said Dillon sarcastically, "you'll allow me time to report officially to Major Ashland, before you take any such vielent steps?"

"Captain," Sebastian said, with equal sarcasm, "I wouldn't for the world interfere with your official duties."

Dillon went on and turned into the bunkhouse where Major Ashland had set up a temporary headquarters. Sam Lester cocked an eye up at Sebastian.

"Now you've had your say about Provo Holt. But how about that man of his, Yance McCloud?"

Sebastian shrugged. "I keep remembering he's Kitty Dutra's brother. Because of that, I've made a lot of allowances for him in the past. But there's a limit to a man's patience. This time he's used up his term of grace. So he leaves, right along with Holt."

Shortly, Captain Judson Dillon reappeared and went back to his party, and there gave orders which started a sorting out of pack animals and the unloading of certain ones, first.

Sebastian murmured, "I've been wanting the chance for a good look at Holt's string, Sam. Here it is, so let's have it."

Ostensibly, they were only idly watching the unpacking chore. In reality they centered a keen interest on every animal in Provo Holt's string. Presently, Ward Sebastian's glance centered on a certain mule just relieved of its burden, an animal which stood a little larger than the rest and which had a split ear.

"Take a look at the big one yonder, Sam. Anything about that one strike you familiar?"

"I suspect there's lots of tall mules with a split-off ear, scattered across the world," answered Sam. "But I doubt any except this one would show a line of white hair on a brown hide, in that exact spot on the point of the near shoulder. I remember Andy Prescott telling me that white hair marked an old snag scar. So, while I ain't a gamblin' man, if I had ten dollars, I'd bet that particular jughead was once lead animal in Andy's

119

string. And if I had another ten, I'd bet the chunky one Yance McCloud's workin' on right now, was more than once rode by Andy Prescott."

"If you didn't take those bets, I would," Sebastian said thinly. "The hell of it is, Sam, while you and I may be dead sure, we can't do much about proving it to others. More than once I tried to get Andy to brand out his whole string. But you know how he was. Happy-go-lucky. Tomorrow is another day."

Sam nodded. "Only," he said succinctly, "for Andy, tomorrow never came."

The unpacking went on, and presently Holt's mules were grouped apart under empty sawbuck saddles. Captain Dillon spoke briefly with Holt, who turned, spat, and stared stonily at Ward Sebastian. Meeting the look, Sebastian moved forward and spoke curtly.

"Don't ever show here again, Holt. Not for any reason or under any pretense. From now on, stay off my land! Yance, that goes for you, too. You keep the wrong kind of company."

Darkly sullen, Yance McCloud said, "I've heard talk that Kitty's here at this ranch. I want to see her."

Sebastian eyed him bleakly. "Not today, Yance. Far as I'm concerned, you've just about run out your string. You've never brought your sister anything but misery and trouble. Knowing Kitty, I know she's not wanting to see you just now. But maybe if you go off somewhere, get yourself an honest job and prove yourself a man, she might feel different. When you've done all that, come back, and we'll talk things over."

120

Provo Holt had stepped into his saddle and was beginning to stir his mules into movement. But before reining completely away he twisted in his saddle and once more laid his pale, cold, always-hating glance on Ward Sebastian.

"So far," he droned, "you've always managed to pick your spots. But one of these days, Sebastian, I'll pick mine! Mark that well. I'll — pick — mine!"

"Like the one picked for Andy Prescott on the Fandango Pass trail, maybe?" charged Sebastian swiftly. "Or the one Jake Ruby tried for me by Sheet Iron?"

Provo Holt gave no answer, moving away.

Captain Judson Dillon came over to Sebastian, his manner stiff and antagonistic.

"As soon as I've cleaned up, I'd like to pay my respects to Miss Ashland. Have I your permission to enter your ranch house, Mister Sebastian?"

"Captain," came the crisp retort, "that's a damn' fool question and you know it. The place is yours. Make yourself at home."

Ward Sebastian spent the balance of the day in his saddle, riding a wide sweep to the east and south of headquarters. Well distant, he came to a big stretch of broken country, a wilderness of gulch and ridge with occasional pockets acres in extent, isolated and hidden among the grim lava rims.

There was good growth in these pockets, and the gulches and draws were tangles of mahogany and cherry brush and wild plum, with now and then a small swamp of quaking aspen. All was browse and graze for cattle and it was good wintering range, for these draws and thickets and rims offered shelter as well as food.

Cattle fed here now, cattle taking on the shagginess of winter coat, and is very fair shape indeed. Cattle carrying Ward Sebastian's plain Square S brand. Here and there he located them, two or three in the draw, half a dozen in that larger gulch yonder, and perhaps a score in the really extensive pocket farther on.

They were wild, scattering for the thickets at his approach, but that was all right. Come spring, they wouldn't be too wild to chouse into the open and drift down to his big basin range around headquarters, for branding and summer feeding. Their wariness now was a fair guarantee of survival through the winter ahead, though invariably the wolves would always get a few and other and always-present range hazards take some additional toll.

He found the spot which old Bob Gayle had told him of, where the Modocs had slow-elked several head. There was little left to mark the place: some scattered bones, a few hoofs, a scrap or two of well-chewed hides, and one half-destroyed skull that the coyotes had worked on and then abandoned.

As he rode, stirring up critters here and there, he made rough count, finding satisfaction in the figures in spite of known losses. It had been a long, slow haul, building up a herd from the frugal start his father had made, but the increase had been steady.

With the gray afternoon running out, he pulled rein on the crest of one of the higher rims, sagged weight in a stirrup and laid a speculative, soberly frowning glance

122

across the far miles to the northeast where, dim in the fading light, a heavy ridge pushed up its blunt-nosed bulk.

Well he knew what that particular ridge looked down on. East of it lay the heart of the lake, while not more than a long rifle shot from the blunt southern point, a savage tangle of lava country began, reaching far south and fanning wide to the west and the east. And the immediate destiny of this part of the world was tied to that wild, rugged area of harsh earth, flinty rock and misty lake waters.

For in the lavas were gathered all the children of old Schonchin, the wise and patient one who, down across the long and wicked years, had asked the white man only for peace and had instead been given oppression; who had signed the white man's treaties as truth and found them lies.

In the lavas now waited Kentipoos — Captain Jack — direct son of Schonchin, with his Modoc brothers. A lost people, who had sent up their prayer smokes, who had listened to their gods, and who were resigned and ready. If their spirits must retreat into the everlasting sunset, then they would go as free spirits. And with them they would take the ghosts of many white men, to carry their burdens for them. So be it . . .

As he reined toward home, Ward Sebastian reached a bleak conclusion. Perhaps it was just as well if a man did not plan too far ahead these days, for, moving across this land as it had now become, he could so suddenly and so easily be dead.

CHAPTER
NINE

By the time Sebastian reached home it was full dark. He met and passed a sentry's challenge and then it was Sam Lester waiting for him.

"You're wanted inside. The womenfolks have kinda laid it on extra-special for supper and I got orders to send you in as soon as you showed. I'll take care of your horse."

"How about you?"

"Already ate. With the troops. You got to know them a little, most of them fellers ain't a bad sort at all. Some are a mite chesty over what they figger to do to the Modocs, but that's because they don't know any better."

Sebastian smiled briefly into the darkness. "Were you younger, Sam, I'd probably lose you to the uniform."

Sam snorted. "Not me! Being my own man suits me fine."

Pausing at the bunkhouse long enough to wash up, Sebastian went into the ranch house. They were gathered about the table in the big kitchen. Connie and Phil Ashland. Major Ashland and Captain Judson Dillon. Mrs. Gayle and Kitty Dutra were busy at the stove.

Major Ashland exclaimed with relief. "Now I feel a little less like a confounded interloper."

"Never feel that way around here, Major," reassured Sebastian quickly.

He took a seat across the table from Connie Ashland and found her regarding him with some gravity. He held her glance, smiling.

"Do I sense a question in you?"

She colored faintly, shaking her head.

Major Ashland, beginning to eat, waved a busy fork.

"You've been in the saddle all afternoon. Fun or business?"

"A little of both," Sebastian said. "I've a fair herd of cattle back in some lava pockets which I consider my winter range. Today was the first opportunity I've had in some time to take a look at them."

"And found everything in good shape, I hope?"

"Good enough. Like everything else, cattle raising has its hazards. But there is also a comforting angle; natural increase is always working."

"I should think, in country like this, you'd lose quite a number to varmints of one sort or another," Phil Ashland remarked.

"Particularly the two-legged kind," put in Captain Dillon. "How about that, Sebastian? Don't the Modocs eat pretty well on any unguarded beef they happen across?"

"Right now, yes. Not very long ago they slow-elked six head of mine. In quieter times, however, they wouldn't touch a single head without my permission, for a number of the Modocs have worked for me, off and on, and know my brand well."

"But this is war, eh, and all obligations of past friendship severed?"

"Call it so."

"Suppose you'd have found some of those very Modocs going after your cattle today," Dillon suggested, "would you have made an argument of it?"

"Certainly."

"A shoot argument?"

"If necessary, yes."

"And they would have shot back?"

"No doubt of it, for that is the kind of world our immediate one has become." Sebastian looked at Dillon with a cool directness. "Captain, I've the feeling you're driving at something else. You are, aren't you?"

Captain Dillon hesitated, then squared his shoulders.

"So long as you ask, yes. I was wondering if you would be as ready to throw a gun on a Modoc Indian as I've twice seen you to be with a person of your own color?"

Before Ward Sebastian could answer, Major Ashland spoke with explosive sharpness.

"Captain, just what are you driving at? I dislike both your tone and your question. Are you forgetting whose house you are in, whose hospitality you're enjoying?"

Sebastian spoke up quickly, the drawl of a sardonic humor in his voice.

"It's all right, Major. Captain Dillon happened to be present on a couple of occasions when I turned a little rough with a certain individual he was doing business with. Perhaps I'd best explain."

"Explain be damned!" growled Major Ashland. "Why should you feel called upon to explain anything to any of us? Captain Dillon, there is an apology due. I want to hear you make it!"

Here was reprimand, blunt and caustic, and it put a flush in Dillon's cheeks and brought a glint to his black eyes. Yet he managed to keep his tone almost suave.

"If an apology is due, consider it rendered."

"No need of one," shrugged Sebastian. "Captain, I take it the person you're referring to is one Provo Holt?"

"That's right."

Sebastian wagged a disapproving head.

"You should never listen to a man like Provo Holt, Captain, let alone believe him. And, all things considered, he'd certainly speak little good of me. But let's get at the meat of this thing. Rightfully, I suppose, any man should have good cause to justify a great hate. I'll give you some reasons for mine."

He paused while his glance ran around the table again, and a mood of soberness came to him.

"I mention briefly the murder of Andy Prescott, a former packer friend of mine. He was found over in the Fandango Pass country, shot in the back, his string of mules gone. Popular opinion laid the blame on some renegade Indians, and it would be useless on my part to try and prove such opinions wrong. Yet I ponder the fact that at least two mules Andy Prescott owned are now in Provo Holt's string."

"You mean the animals can be identified by a brand of some sort?" Dillon asked.

Sebastian shook his head. "The animals are not branded."

"Then how can you possibly be sure of their former ownership?"

"Certain markings or scars, such as a split ear on one of them. Shades of coloration help, too, or just the over-all appearance of an animal will do. Any man, much around mules, develops a sort of instinct for recognition of them."

Dillon scoffed. "That's mighty flimsy evidence on which to accuse a man of murder and robbery. It wouldn't hold for a minute in any fair court of law."

"That's right," agreed Sebastian dryly, "it wouldn't. Which is the reason I've never offered it in one, however certain I might be myself. But suppose we pass over that matter and consider something of which there can be no possible doubt, for this I saw with my own eyes."

He lifted the coffee cup at his elbow, drank of it, then seemed to retreat far off by himself as he stared across the rim of the cup at a past memory which turned his look dark and brooding. He began slowly.

"A small group of Modocs, mainly squaws and children and very old men, were camped at Desolation Flat. They, along with others, had fled the Klamath Reservation because of the persecution inflicted on them by the Klamaths, their hereditary enemies, who greatly outnumbered them. A detachment of militia, along with some civilian volunteers, was sent out to

128

round up these fugitives and take them back to the reservation. Among the civilian volunteers was this fellow Provo Holt and another like him, one Jake Ruby.

"I was returning from a trip to the Pit River country. I came in at Desolation Flat just as the trouble broke. The officer in charge of the militia later acknowledged that no cause for gun work existed at all. But there had always been a willingness by some to open up on an Indian at any excuse, or none at all, for that matter. At any rate, some of the civilian volunteers started shooting."

Aroused feeling flared sharply in Sebastian's eyes and his words rang bleakly.

"I doubt I'll ever forget the rest of it. I saw one of these civilians, Jake Ruby, deliberately shoot down a very old and stone-blind Modoc elder. Then there was a squaw, young and rather pretty. She had a papoose in her arms, a mite of a thing but a few days old. She could have been any one of all the young mothers in this world. She was frightened and she ran, hunting safety for her baby and herself. Whatever the ancient cause of hostility between red man and white, certainly she was in no way at fault. Neither did she understand. She just ran, holding her baby. And while she ran, this Provo Holt, this acquaintance of yours, Captain Dillon, shot her. She fell right in front of me, her eyes full of a great, unbelieving terror and a haunting reproach as she died."

Sebastian hit his feet, took a turn up and down the room, unable to remain still under the lash of the wicked memory. Over his shoulder he added a final few words.

"The papoose was caught under its mother as she fell. It did not live long after that."

Major Ross Ashland cleared his throat savagely.

"You should have shot that damned scoundrel on the spot!"

"I would have," Sebastian said flatly, "but others in the party got between us. Since then, I've tried again and again to force both Provo Holt and Jake Ruby to a show-down. But both of them know what I'm after and keep backing away."

He came to an abrupt stop in his pacing and stared down at Judson Dillon.

"Well, Captain, have I answered your question?"

Captain Dillon's reply was subdued. "Yes. Almost too well."

Sebastian put his glance on Connie Ashland. Her face was pale, her eyes glistening with welling tears. She was watching him steadily. He touched his wounded left arm.

"You asked me who was responsible for this. I'll name him now. Jake Ruby. He tried to gulch me at Sheet Iron Butte. I told you it wasn't a pretty story." His tone gentled. "I'm sorry if I've upset you."

She shook her head, her answer low and muffled.

"It's all right — all right."

The Siskiyou house stood on Miner Street, almost directly opposite Jeff Chesbro's big store and trading post. Ward Sebastian, back in Yreka after some two

130

weeks of absence, crossed to the hotel and went in, nodding to the clerk at the desk.

"You're holding a trunk belonging to Miss Constance Ashland?"

"Yes. It was supposed to be picked up by the military. Nobody has called for it yet."

"I'll take if off your hands tomorrow. Miss Ashland has authorized me to bring it on to her."

"What's this? What's this?" The voice was at Sebastian's elbow. "Did I hear you say you were hauling luggage for a lady?"

It was Harley Ritter. He was his usual freshly shaven, pink-cheeked, fragrant self. Sebastian looked down, the beginning of a frown of annoyance darkening his face. Then, as he rubbed a hand across his own weather-roughened, unshaven jaw, the frown turned into a half-smiling, sardonic tolerance.

"Harley, why do you always have to be so damn' prettied up? You make me feel like a tramp."

Harley shrugged plump shoulders. "In my business a man has to keep up appearances. But what is this about a young lady's trunk? What young lady?"

"A quite attractive one," Sebastian told him dryly. "Miss Ashland. She was on her way to Fort Klamath, but military necessity blocked that plan. So, for the present she is a guest at my ranch. Tell me, how's the junior partner making out? How's law — and crime? They more or less go together, don't they?"

Harley's eyes narrowed a trifle as though he was not entirely sure but that a touch of ironic sarcasm lay behind Sebastian's seemingly casual questions. Even so, he could not refrain from swelling a bit with importance.

"We've plenty to do, Mr. Biglow and I. There are some hints that Mr. Biglow may be called upon to set up proceedings of arbitration between the government and those damned Modocs."

"Too late for that," declared Sebastian flatly. "Much too late. Successful arbitration requires some degree of trust, and those damned Modocs, as you call them, have long since found out, to their bitter cost, that it doesn't pay to trust the white man. No, Harley, there'll be no arbitration."

"That suits me," Ritter said. "I'm sick and tired of any and all mawkish concern for the Modocs. Clean them out, I say, once and for all. Get rid of the whole filthy lot of them. They're not worth wasting time or sympathy on!"

Sebastian looked the rotund lawyer over with chilling glance, and his tone went crisp.

"Harley, I've heard you say that before. You're a blood-thirsty little bastard, aren't you?"

Crimson suffused Harley Ritter's well-fed cheeks. A glitter hardened his eyes and shrillness sharpened his voice.

"Who are you to talk? Can't you do anything but take the part of those useless stinking savages? What kind of a white man are you, anyhow?"

Ward Sebastian watched Harley Ritter swell and crimson with anger, saw the streak of inherent meanness in the man rise and display itself. Abruptly he dropped all pretense of friendliness or geniality.

"Not your kind, Ritter," he said, his words flat with distaste. "For which, I thank God! Now get out of my way before I step on you!"

He brushed past and moved out into the street, to be met there by a mist-laden wind coming in off the Siskiyous, a wind swollen with the vitality of this wild land round about. On it rode the odor of rain-drenched timber, the vigor of rocky peaks cleansed and chilled by driving snow blizzards, and all the raw, rich flavors of the earth itself, undergoing the ever-resurgent alchemy of the changing seasons.

He turned downstreet, a tall free-striding figure, unconsciously reveling in all which the wind was bringing to him, for these were vital ingredients of the freedom that he valued as he did his life

The afternoon was fading, a deepening gloom washing through the town. Lights were already burning in various buildings, pushing their pale yellow glow out of mist-fogged windows.

The door of Curt Dennison's Timberlodge Bar swung back, letting out a couple of bearded miners, and with them came a gust of warm air, the mixed breath of tobacco and whisky and the wet woolen clothes of men. It was earthy and real and human, and Sebastian turned into the place, the pull of a keening anticipation on his face.

The saloon was well filled, but Sebastian found a place at the bar and Curt Dennison brought bottle and glasses.

"Ward, this is the first time in months, seems like. Man, where you been?"

133

Sebastian grinned. "Name any spot between the coast and Nevada, or between Oregon and the big valley down-state, and chances are I've been there, Curt. It's a big chunk of country."

He spun a dollar on the bar, bought some cigars, poured a drink and invited Dennison to join him. Old friends, they lifted their glasses to each other and put the whisky away. After which, Dennison poured one on the house before moving down the bar to answer the insistence of a pair of thirsty ones. Sebastian lighted a cigar, savoring its fragrance as he dawdled over his second drink.

Intervals such as this, he mused, were good for a man, kept him from going sour. A couple of drinks, a cigar, and time to wring the flavor from both — things as simple as these had their good place in a man's life and made it richer.

What with the day-long, stored-up warmth of this crowded bar, and the heat of the whisky now beginning to work, he tipped back his hat and opened his coat. He ran a reflective hand across his whiskery jaw for a second time and decided he'd have to shave before dropping in on Anne Biglow this night.

He'd done a lot of thinking about Anne along the two-day drag in from the ranch. The way they had parted the last time, and the reason behind it, had left him uneasy. There had been the makings of a quarrel, and probably the fault was his. For the roughness of this land he lived so close to was in him, and could grate on the sensibilities of anyone who had been raised softly and securely, as Anne had.

He put his second drink away, considered a third, decided against it and started to turn from the bar. Then he froze all movement under the impact of the words that reached him.

"You were lucky at Sheet Iron, Sebastian. You won't be, here!"

The tone was wicked, the intent deadly.

The voice was Jake Ruby's.

The man at Ward Sebastian's left cried thinly:

"Christ! He's throwing a gun!"

A few times before in his life, Sebastian had found that a man's reactions during moments of extreme danger or urgency were not necessarily product of his conscious will. At such times sheer instinct could take over. It was so now.

Instinct as fine and bright as a silver thread cut through the first startled awareness. He wasted no time trying to turn or look. He simply flung himself hard and desperately against the man on his left, catching him off balance, knocking him sprawling.

The report of Jake Ruby's gun was a dull and stunning blast, and the bullet from it crashed into the bar where Ward Sebastian had been standing but a split second before.

The bellow of that shot did things to men in the room. Some it startled to immobility, others it stampeded. A teamster, downbar a couple of yards, was one of these. Already well along in his liquor and understanding nothing but the implied import of a gun's trapped roar, he let out a bewildered yell and charged wildly for the door. In passing, his burly shoulder clipped Jack Ruby, spinning him completely around, and blocking Ruby's chance for a second easy try at Sebastian.

On his part, still moving to the left under the impetus of that first desperate lunge, Ward Sebastian was dragging at his gun and whirling to face the threat that had come up so treacherously behind him. The legs of the man he'd upset were thrashing wildly and he stumbled over these and went down to one knee, and from this position looked up into Jake Ruby's contorted face.

From his knee, just as he was, Sebastian got away his shot, driving it upward at his target, knowing it had to count, and that he'd not get a second chance. He saw Jake Ruby roll up on his toes as the impact of the slug lifted him. He saw agony strike across the man's twisted features, then swiftly fade as all expression loosened and went slackly away.

Jake Ruby fell on his face, soddenly, heavily.

Came a long breath of aching silence, then the barroom turned into bedlam, men yelling and cursing and pushing about, some trying to get farther away from the dead man on the floor, some trying to come up for a closer look. Ward Sebastian, lifting erect, backed against the bar, feet spread and shoulders swung forward as he stared down at the huddled figure of Jake Ruby.

The man he'd driven into and knocked off his feet now scrambled up, white and shaky. Tone husky in his throat, Sebastian said:

136

"Sorry, friend. Didn't mean to upset you. But I had no other out."

"What the hell!" was the reply. "He was throwing a gun, wasn't he? All set to shoot you in the back? I don't know yet how he missed!"

The door of the place swung open and Dick Brace came pushing in ahead of several other curious ones, among them Harley Ritter. Brace was a medium-sized man with a blunt jaw and steady eyes. He was marshal of the town.

Men gave back, made an open lane between the marshal and the dead man on the floor. Brace stared, moved quickly forward and bent for a brief examination. He straightened and put his glance on Sebastian, who still held a naked gun in his hand.

"You?"

Sebastian nodded. "I'm at the bar, just finished with a drink. He came up behind me, set to finish me. If he hadn't stopped to talk about it, he'd have made it good. But he wanted me to know who it was that gunned me down. That gave me a long chance. I was so lucky I still don't believe it!"

Curt Dennison came up behind the bar and Dick Brace turned to him.

"How did you see it, Dennison?"

"Exactly as Sebastian says." Dennison reached across the bar and gripped Sebastian's arm. "Man, you got no idea how happy I am to see you on your feet, not down there on the floor!"

Dick Brace had another look at Jake Ruby, then turned again to Sebastian.

"What was between you two? Why should he have been after you?"

"A long story. It doesn't particularly matter, does it?"

The marshal regarded him speculatively, then shrugged.

"Considering how it happened, I guess not."

Sebastian nodded, put his gun away and went out, the crowd opening to let him pass, looking at him with a mixture of expressions. Regardless of the complete justification of the act, he'd just killed a man and that marked him.

The rush of the wet wind was good in his face. He leaned into it, sucking its wild vigor deep into his lungs. He had the feeling that it was a clean current washing all through him.

His left shoulder was aching a little, the left shoulder and arm, the wounded one. He had driven it violently against the man who had stood beside him at the bar. But even as he acknowledged it, the pain was lessening. The wound had healed well.

The scar, of course, he'd carry all his life. That was the mark Jake Ruby had put on him. But now Jake Ruby lay dead on the floor of the Timberlodge, his account fully totaled, the balance struck.

Recounting what could have happened and what did happen, Sebastian wondered how much destiny had to do with the lives and fortunes of men.

Men came out of the Timberlodge. Harley Ritter came out. He stopped beside Ward Sebastian, peering up at him, grimacing his dislike.

"How does it feel to have a dead man on your hands?" It was a shrill, almost yapping taunt. "How does it feel, Sebastian?"

Silently Sebastian regarded this man, completely despising him. He put a spread hand against Ritter's chest, gave him a shove that sent him reeling. After which, bending his head into the wind, Sebastian moved away.

CHAPTER
TEN

There was strain in the atmosphere of the gabled house on upper Oregon Street, and Ward Sebastian sensed it the moment he entered the place. Anne Biglow had opened the door to his knock, but her worded greeting was stiff and vaguely distant, and by the time he'd shucked his coat she was at the far end of the hall, stepping into the living room.

Moving through a gray depression since the shoot-out in the Timberlodge, he had been almost boyishly eager for a warm and understanding greeting, and now he knew biting disappointment.

This was not lessened in any way when he followed Anne into the big room, for Harley Ritter occupied an easy chair before the fire, a freshly lighted perfecto between his teeth. Ritter's only move to acknowledge Sebastian's entrance was to throw a quick glance that carried a hard, antagonistic glint. Anne, moving to the far end of the hearth, put Ritter and his chair between Sebastian and herself.

This could have been an entirely meaningless move, but to Sebastian it seemed significant and a gust of feeling compounded of his depression and the raw cut of disappointment whipped through him. Out of this

140

came recklessness and a quickening temper. He looked at Ritter and put the lash of words on him.

"Harley, when a lady enters the room with another guest, a gentleman gets to his feet. Or maybe you didn't read that far in your book of manners?"

Instantly livid, Ritter made as if to rise. Anne Biglow dropped a hand on his shoulder, pushing him back. She faced Sebastian accusingly.

"Ward, that was deliberately insulting. Please remember where you are!"

"I am remembering and perhaps beginning to wonder why I came. Maybe I made a mistake, showing up. Why not give it to me straight, Anne — am I welcome or not?"

She faltered a little before this blunt directness.

"Why, why of course you are welcome. But do you have to start a quarrel the moment you step into the house?"

"The quarrel, my dear," he said, "started a long time ago. It started the day Ritter and I first laid eyes on each other. Now we have taken off the gloves. He hates my soul, and I've nothing but contempt for him. I wish he'd take the hint and clear out. He's spoiling what I'd hoped would be a pleasant evening for you and me. And I could use a pleasant evening after as rough a day as I've been through."

Harley Ritter, making no move toward leaving, spoke up.

"I imagine that any day you kill a man, Sebastian, could turn out to be a rough one."

141

Watching, Sebastian saw the color fade from Anne's cheeks.

"Harley," he said, coldly soft, "you've been telling things about me. Are you sure you told them right?"

"Jake Ruby's dead, isn't he?" came the taunting retort. "And if you didn't kill him, who did?"

Sebastian looked at Anne again, his words all for her.

"If the right of extreme necessity hadn't been on my side, Anne, then Dick Brace would have me behind bars right now."

She stared into the fire. "I don't care to think about it. If you say you had to do it, I believe you."

The words were there, but they carried no conviction or warmth of understanding, and as he weighed them, cynicism took root in Sebastian.

"I'm glad you believe me, Anne. But I wonder how long you'll remember it? Maybe too long. Maybe all the rest of your life. Not as something that had to be, but as something I did. Think on it, Anne. For of a sudden I find I have to know, and surely!"

The tone, the stern impact of his words, brought her quickly around to face him.

"What do you mean, Ward? What are you driving at? I don't believe I understand."

The demand had come off his lips almost involuntarily and was, to a degree, as startling to him as to her. But now, considering it, he knew it reflected his exact intention and desire.

He knew also that he was forever done with entering this house in apology. As a man fashioned to the needs and ways of the wild land he moved through, if the

142

necessity to kill came up, that was just the way the trail ran. He might regret the necessity, but he'd not apologize for the act.

How about Anne, though? How long would she remember, and with revulsion? If even for a day, then there was no hope of lasting happiness between them at all. Now, speaking slowly and gravely, he brought this issue fully into the open.

"Anne, you and I have been aimlessly marking time, more or less playing at make believe, and I see neither point nor sense to such any longer. It's high time we faced realities. Either there is something worthwhile ahead for the pair of us, or there isn't. And tonight I want to know about that — for certain!"

Here was a thing Anne Biglow had come to fear, the time for decision and certainty between this big, rugged man and herself. Yes or no! And either way with finality. Always she had known there was a chance that he might stampede her against all considered judgment, for in him there was a power and a sweep of emotion that could easily kindle an answering flame.

There was, in Anne Biglow, a streak of calculating materialism, and outright decision in anything was something she never wished to give unless it suited her exactly reasoned desire. So now, instead of answering Sebastian's question, she took refuge in one of her own.

"You've been saying what you want to know. Very well, this is what I want to know. Who is Constance Ashland, and what is your interest in her? What is she doing at your ranch?"

Sebastian considered her intently while his lips pulled to a shadowy, mirthless, cynical smile. It was the look of one who had found disillusionment.

For in Anne Biglow's question he'd found the answer to his. She had neatly side-stepped and, looking back over their relationship from its very beginnings, he could see where she had always been adept at side-stepping obligations and decisions. And she would never change, for in her there lay selfishness and an inherent evasiveness. To the eye she would be her small and perfect self. But in the many things that really counted, she was empty.

Sebastian turned and put his glance on Harley Ritter.

"Carrying still other tales, eh, Harley? And you didn't tell this one right either, did you?"

In Harley Ritter's answering shrug there was a smug mockery.

"No need for you to squirm, Sebastian — providing everything is on the square."

Abrupt harshness blazed in Sebastian. "You contempt- ible little whelp! Watch that loose mouth of yours or I'll shake some manners into you!"

"Ward!" reminded Anne sharply. "You haven't answered me."

He turned to her again and, though the shadow of that mirthless smile touched his lips once more, there was a cold judgment in his eyes that made her shrink.

"My dear," he said evenly, "I came here tonight fully intending to tell you all about Miss Constance Ashland. Now I won't bother. For I can't remember when I've

144

come into this house without having to explain or apologize or beg forgiveness for some damned thing or another. And if I bowed my head abjectly enough I'd be rewarded with your smile and the touch of your hand or, on rare occasions perhaps, by a kiss. But it was certain to be a cautious one, wary and resisting, never fully and warmly given. Anne, that just isn't my idea of a good life, and never could be."

Now the recklessness in him was fully on the loose, and his smile became a curt laugh.

"Once I held to what I thought was a good hope. But no longer. Yet the hope deserves a final accolade before being laid away in sackcloth and ashes. You needn't be afraid of this kiss, Anne — because it is the last one!"

He was swiftly close to her and with his arms around her. She seemed too stunned to either answer or resist, and there was nothing in her lips at all.

But now there were hands pulling and clawing at him. Harley Ritter's hands. And there was Harley Ritter's voice sounding, shrill with a jealous fury.

"Leave her alone, damn you! Leave her alone!"

Sebastian put Anne aside and turned, hunching a shoulder against Ritter to hold him off.

"Why Harley!" he exclaimed. "What's come over you? Where did you ever rake up the nerve?"

Ritter came charging back, completely beside himself. His teeth were bared, his soft, barbered cheeks suffused, his eyes crazily ablaze. He struck no blows, but instead kept clawing at Sebastian like an enraged cat. And, catlike, he got a hand past a warding arm and dragged slicing fingernails across Sebastian's jaw, scarring it with smarting furrows. Another clawing grab missed Sebastian's eyes by inches only.

Sebastian hit him then, a swinging slap with his open hand. The hard, rope- and rein-calloused palm caught Ritter across the mouth and nose with enough startled anger behind it to knock him back into the easy chair, where he crouched, dazed but still snarling, a line of crimson beginning to seep from his cuffed nose.

Sebastian, fingering his clawed jaw, put his glance on Anne Biglow as she stood, white of face and very still. Honest regret gentled his words.

"This is a hell of a way for anything to end, Anne. For my part I'm both sorry and ashamed. Good-by!"

As the sound of the closing front door marked Ward Sebastian's certain departure, Anne shifted to face the hearth, her small shoulders sagging as she covered her face with her hands. Harley Ritter, dabbing at his nose with a handkerchief, went over to her and tried to put a comforting arm about her.

"It's all right, Anne, all right! You're well rid of him. He never was your kind, never was good enough for you." Ritter's voice was still shrill with emotion.

She seemed not to hear him, for she gave him no answer. And at the touch of his arm she whirled away and ran from the room.

At the Sebastian ranch the ominous gruel of war's sure threat was steadily thickening. Troops from Yreka, along with their slow-toiling wagons of supply, came through in increasing numbers, to camp for a night on the wide acres of the basin, then move on into the east. Dispatch riders raced in and spurred away again. All of this quickening activity built a deepening sense of anxiety in Constance Ashland.

She began worrying about her menfolks, for Captain Jud Dillon had already been called ahead, word coming back that Colonel Frank Wheaton, commanding the forward area, had made Dillon his adjutant. How long before brother Phil and Uncle Ross would be called up too? She began to fear and hate that gray, misted world to the east.

She had heard talk of the great, sprawling lake out there. Tule Lake, men called it, where the wildfowl swarmed beyond all counting. Then there was the land that touched the lower end of the lake and spread far to the south of it. This stretch men spoke of as "the lava beds," and to Connie the name carried strong hint of a cruel and savage land.

In an additional way, she worried about her brother. For young Lieutenant Phil Ashland and Kitty Dutra were showing more than a casual interest in each other. At first it had been just an exchange of glances, with open admiration in Phil's eyes and a quiet smiling by Kitty Dutra. Then, on some pretense or other, Phil began dropping in at the ranch house more and more often, when always his glance would eagerly seek out the dark, quiet young widow and he would find some cause to speak to her.

Once Connie saw them together by the kitchen door, their voices running low, the two of them completely oblivious to all around them. When Phil walked away he was whistling, while Kitty Dutra looked after him with shadowed eyes and that grave, quiet smile. In her irritation over the incident, Connie failed to note the soft, soft glow shining far back in Kitty Dutra's eyes. Phil, Connie told herself, was such a boy, and with all his future ahead of him.

She set out to remind him of this one evening and was startled and dismayed when he stopped her abruptly, looking very mature and determined.

"Whoa-up, Connie! I know what you're driving at and it won't do. I don't mind you fussing over me a little if it makes you happy, but in some things you'll not interfere, and this is one of them. I'm a man grown, not a little boy. You must quit thinking of me as such."

"But, Phil, she's older. And a widow. And —"

"She's younger than me by a year," Phil cut in. "A widow, yes. But still just a girl, who, from what Ward Sebastian has said, has found damned little happiness in life. It happens, Connie, that I see Kitty Dutra as a very wonderful person, so don't make me quarrel with you over that fact!"

After which, Connie set out to thoroughly dislike Kitty Dutra and without any great success, for Kitty met chill and stiffness with warmth and kindness, tendering the hand of friendship shyly, fearful of rejection. So, fundamentally honest, Connie had to admit to depths of sweetness in Kitty she had not guessed at before. In the end she decided to withhold judgment.

Through the slow, cold grayness of another early winter morning, a dispatch rider spurred in from the east and set his mount to a steaming halt at the door of

148

Major Ashland's bunkhouse headquarters. Five minutes later, Phil Ashland came quickly to the ranch house.

The mutter of those racing, incoming hoofs had brought Connie to a window. When she saw Phil hurrying across to the house, a quickening tension rose in her. Turning, she found Kitty Dutra beside her, and in Kitty's eyes was a worry to match her own.

Phil was all exultant eagerness. "We're going up! At last there's the real business of a soldier ahead."

"You — you and Uncle Ross, too?" Connie tried to keep the tremor from her voice.

"Everybody," affirmed Phil. "Now! Things to do!"

Within an hour troops were leaving the ranch, taking that lonely road to the east. Finally, but one last wagon remained. Major Ashland came over to the house, bowed over the hands of Mrs. Gayle and Kitty Dutra, put an arm about Connie and brushed her cheek with his lips. The saltiness of a stray tear was on that cheek and the major spoke with gentle gruffness.

"Now — now! No tears, youngster. Everything will be all right."

"You'll keep an eye on Phil, Uncle Ross? He's so eager to prove himself. He could be reckless —"

"I'll keep him curbed," promised the major. "So, keep that chin high and brave. Remember, you're of the Army too."

He went out, a solid, dependable soldier, never destined for greatness, but owning the comforting knowledge that it was his efforts, and those of many like him, that brought greatness to the exalted few.

When Phil came in again, he had shed his first exuberance, was now gravely sober. He thanked Mrs. Gayle for all her care and kindness. He held Connie tightly, chiding her with soft affection when her tears began getting away from her. Then he turned to Kitty Dutra, who stood utterly still by the window, her dark eyes fixed unwaveringly on this tall, clean-faced young soldier.

It seemed to Connie that neither of these two intent people moved so much as a finger for a long minute. Then Phil stepped forward and Kitty came swiftly to meet him and his open arms.

Mrs. Gayle touched Connie and they went quietly out, leaving these two alone.

Half an hour later, steady and herself again, Connie was in her room. There was soft movement at the door and Kitty Dutra came in. She stood, hands folded in front of her, looking at Connie.

"You don't approve, do you?" she said quietly.

"Would it make any difference, either way?"

"Of course," Kitty said simply. "I so deeply want you to approve. I know what you are thinking. That I am a widow, whose husband not very long ago met violent death at the hands of the Modocs. So, I should be deep-sunk in depths of mourning, unable to even look at another man. That, no doubt, is what custom decrees. But sometimes life has a way of marching right over custom. Do — do you mind listening?"

"Not at all."

"Thank you. Suppose," Kitty went on, "that I told you my marriage to Nick Dutra was the headlong folly

150

of a desperate girl, so frantic to get away from the brutal environment of a drunken father and a renegade brother, she never fully considered what another might hold. I — I found out, all right. I stayed with Nick Dutra because I'd made a bargain. But more and more came the feeling that we were really strangers, and I know that toward the end he felt the same.

"Quite naturally, word of Nick's death shocked me, and I was deeply sorry. But I found I could not truly mourn him. You see, Connie, I'm being shamelessly honest about this. We mourn where love has truly been, but where it hasn't, why there just isn't anything to mourn. Again, custom may say we should, but if we do we're hypocrites. And I've never been such."

Facing her, Connie did not answer for a moment, marveling at the change she saw. Where, when first met, there had been something not far from cynical hardness armoring Kitty Dutra, now there was a softness, a gentleness which made her seem very young and hesitant, asking poignantly for understanding. Under Connie's searching scrutiny, Kitty's glance never wavered.

"Knowing Phil," Connie said gravely, "I know how completely real and unselfish it will be with him. Will it be the same with you, Kitty?"

Kitty's dark eyes were suddenly bright with tears, her lips quivering, her voice husky with feeling.

"I — I wouldn't be here talking to you if there was even the slightest chance of it being less than that. Can you look at me and doubt me, Connie?"

151

In a softening rush of understanding, Connie held out her arms.

"Why then," she said, none too steady herself, "I'm glad, Kitty. And truly!"

That evening Ward Sebastian and Sam Lester brought the loaded pack string in at the ranch.

With day running out, Connie Ashland had donned her blue cloak and left the ranch house, determined to seek a little freedom and movement to still her stirred-up emotions.

Pacing up and down, she had watched dusk come in across the world, swallowing up the distant buttes, one by one, then shrouding the nearer rims and finally closing out all but the immediate area close at hand. And then, through this chill and deepening gloom, there came the plodding pack train, with Sam Lester riding out ahead, and the bell of the lead mule making a small, tinkling melody.

Old Bob Gayle tramped over to open a corral gate and Connie stole that way herself, startled at the stir of eagerness she knew at this arrival. She heard Bob Gayle say something to Sam Lester, and clearly caught Sam's answer.

"No trouble at all along the trail. But at the Timberlodge Bar in town, hell bust loose. Jake Ruby came up in back of Ward, threw a gun. He was aiming to get Ward without giving Ward a chance. But Ward killed him in the shoot-out. Don't say anything about it. Ward's plenty low in mood. He ain't spoke twenty words since we pulled out of Yreka yesterday mornin'."

152

"But he did kill Jake Ruby?" Bob Gayle's voice climbed with excitement.

"He killed him, all right."

"Damned good riddance!" old Bob said flatly. "That evens up some for the dirty business at Desolation Flat."

Just voices in the chill dusk, passing words back and forth that reached Connie Ashland's ears. Then full understanding of the content of the words began to strike home.

A man had been killed. A man named Jake Ruby. And Ward Sebastian had killed him!

Connie's eyes grew big as the picture took form in her mind. A saloon in Yreka. Violence — the gunfire kind of violence which left a dead man on the floor. Killed by Ward Sebastian . . .

She went quietly back to the ranch house, to her room. And there she stayed until she heard the deeper voices of men in the kitchen and Kitty Dutra came to call her to supper.

Her first glance was for Sebastian. He stood over by the stove, his hands behind him. His big shoulders sagged and he was quiet and withdrawn. He stirred as Connie came in, glanced at her briefly, murmured "Good evening. Your trunk is here." Then he went off again into his locked-away thoughts.

He kept within the same mood when they sat at the table, eating mechanically, saying nothing. Several times Connie found herself staring furtively at his hands. Powerful, work-toughened, weather-darkened. They had only recently killed a man. She shivered slightly.

153

Abruptly, she took herself to task. Who was she to judge, one way or another? For this was that kind of a land; a harsh land and cruel, charged with all the elements that could lead to raw violence. A land where men had to fashion themselves to its demands, else they did not long endure.

When hungry men ate, a meal could be soon done with. Ward Sebastian pushed back his chair, reached for his pipe, and for the first time spoke out of his mood, looking at old Bob Gayle.

"Sam and I go on in the morning, Bob. The supplies are for Homer Shadworth, over in Surprise Valley. I'm hoping to meet Bill Wiggin at Jack Hume's place and have him take the stuff on from there. But if I can't locate him, then Sam and I will have to go on across the Warners, and time could run into a couple of weeks before we get back."

Food, the solace of tobacco and this break in his silent mood seemed to loosen him up and mellow him, for when Sam Lester and Bob Gayle went out to take care of some final chores, he lingered and addressed himself to Connie.

"You're being well cared for?"

"Much too well and much too kindly," she assured him. "And I've been making friends with your books. You don't mind?"

"Mind?" His eyes brightened. "Just the opposite. Lately I've neglected them. Some are rather good, don't you think?"

"Very good," Connie said.

"The older ones were my father's. He brought them with him across the plains He would crouch by the campfire at night, poring over one of them. Some in the party were inclined to scoff, but he was the strongest, most capable one of them all."

"He must have been a remarkable man," Connie encouraged.

"All of that," Sebastian nodded, his tone going gentle with remembrance. "Why, I recall one time —"

A little haltingly at first, almost self-consciously, the words came. But gradually he eased and settled back in his chair, while one reminiscence led to another and still another until it became a dam of pent-up feeling giving way. Watching, listening, Connie Ashland understood.

She realized that there was in this man, long denied, a need for expression and understanding. Happenings of strong emotional impact — not the least of which was the shooting affair back in Yreka — had driven him into a corner by himself, where he had crouched in loneliness. Unconsciously seeking release, he now, in her interest, found it.

Neither of them were aware when, finished with the dishes, Mrs. Gayle and Kitty Dutra quietly left the room. Sebastian, his pipe gone cold, talked on and on, while the set of harshness edging his face and the shadow of bleakness which lay far back in his eyes, softened and went away.

He caught himself up finally, showing something not far from consternation.

"Good Lord! How I've been going on! Why didn't you shut me up?" He shook his head as though bewildered. "I don't understand what came over me to have punished you with all that talk."

She smiled at him, slightly misty of eye. "The need was in you. I've been fascinated."

He got to his feet, shaking his head again. "I'm not usually given to running on like that. In fact, I can't ever remember another time when I gave way so."

"Not realizing it," Connie murmured, "you've just paid me the nicest compliment I've ever known."

He looked at her with a great new interest, seeing her as never before. He had known that she was fair and fine to look upon, that there was strength and resolution in her. And courage. Now he saw more. He saw complete honesty and a deep womanliness, despite her girlish years. He saw a spirit and a warmth of understanding that could hold a man together and give him the will to challenge the world. Gravely he spoke.

"You understood, didn't you? And I needed that."

He moved to the door and her words followed him.

"You spoke of it casually, of heading east into the lake and lava country in the morning. I've come to have a deep fear of that place. Take care of yourself."

He paused for a moment in the doorway, the rawly bitter breath of the night rushing in past him. His glance lay on her intently. There was no slightest hint of coquetry in her, no attempt to play on his emotions one way or another. Nothing but sincere good wishes for his journey. Her eyes were gray and faultlessly clear to their

156

very depths, and her lips curved in a faint, sweet smiling.

He nodded and nodded again.

"Yes, you do understand. Stay long with us, Constance Ashland. Stay long with us!"

CHAPTER
ELEVEN

Colonel Frank Wheaton was a gaunt, loosely-put-together man with deep-set eyes and the long, sober face of a scholar. Under lowering skies he stood on the lifting slope of rocky earth below the point of a blunt-nosed ridge and, minutely and with care, surveyed the sweep of country running south and west. Lowering his field glasses he turned to the officer at his elbow.

"Dillon, I don't like it any better than I did the first time I looked at it."

Captain Judson Dillon, lean and taut and with smoky black eyes, stirred restlessly.

"They won't attack, so we have to. And it will soon be over."

Colonel Wheaton shook his head. "I'd like to share your confidence, but I don't. What do you see on that land out there? Just a sweep of sage and other brush, scabbed here and there with the bones of ancient lava. And apparently lifeless. But when you watch closely, you see that it isn't lifeless. Here and there a thin stain of woodsmoke seeps up, seemingly out of the very earth itself.

"Modoc Indians are out there, Dillon; Kentipoos — Captain Jack and his people. We don't see them, but they're there. And when we attack they'll still be there, and we won't see them. But they will see us, and only too well! No, I don't like it."

Captain Dillon twitched impatient shoulders. "How many of them, Colonel — against our hundreds?"

"Something between fifty and sixty, according to my scout advices. However, military history is full of instances where a handful of brave and desperate men, fighting from a position of their own choosing, have exacted wicked toll of an attacking force far superior in numbers. I tell you I've a feeling about this affair, and I don't like it."

"But we do attack?"

Colonel Wheaton flashed a swift glance at his companion, as though sensing a shadow of rebuke in the question. His eyes chilled slightly and his words ran curt.

"Certainly. I may not always approve of my orders, but I follow them." He paused and, being innately a kindly man, his tone mellowed.

"You've never been thoroughly blooded, Dillon. The fault is in no way your own, of course. You're just so damned efficient with forms and figures, with regulations and procedure, you've always drawn staff or logistical duty. And made an enviable reputation for yourself, I might add.

"But a certain routine, strictly adhered to, tends to fashion a man's thinking. Like seeing a written order and accepting its intrinsic worth too blindly. For let him start translating that order into the human factor and he can find himself abruptly — and frighteningly — dealing with the lives of other men."

Again Colonel Wheaton paused, the gravity of his face deepening.

"There," he said slowly, "you face a responsibility that can haunt you. The lives of your men, their blood, their agony, all in your hands. At such times it is easy to doubt your own judgment and that of your superiors. But, being a professional soldier, you accept your orders and you obey them. I've been ordered to attack. I do so, in the morning!"

Colonel Wheaton took another long, brooding look at the sprawling, broken plain of sage and harsh earth and harsher lava, running out into a gray, misted distance where scattered buttes hunched sullen shoulders. After which he led the way off the slope, down to a flat where an orderly waited with horses.

Short of midday, Ward Sebastian and Sam Lester brought their pack string in at Henry Gallatin's ranch. The place was jammed with troops, furious with activity. Uniformed men were everywhere, working at a thousand details. Supply wagons that had creaked their way in from Yreka, or down from Fort Klamath and Linkville, were parked in tired lines, some empty, some being unloaded.

A troop of the First Cavalry, hard-bitten, hard-riding, just in from Fort Bidwell over past the Warner Mountains, were setting up a picket line. Army mules

160

and horses were eating deep into Henry Gallatin's supply of winter hay.

Leaving Sam Lester to hold back the pack string, Ward Sebastian went ahead and sought out the grizzled, stocky, stern-eyed owner of the ranch. To Sebastian's question, Henry Gallatin nodded.

"Bill Wiggin is waiting for you at Vinegar Spring. Too much fuss going on around here to suit him. He's anxious for the supplies for Homer Shadworth."

"I got them for him." Sebastian considered the military activity all around about, then added soberly, "What do you make of it, Henry?"

Gallatin shrugged.

"I don't like it. But there is nothing I can do about it. I started out damning the military, then realized that didn't make a lick of sense. They got to do what Washington tells them to do. Colonel Wheaton — he's in command right now — is a very decent sort, a good man. But he's not enjoying the chore ahead one damned bit."

Sebastian stirred restlessly.

"How far back does Modoc tribal history run, Henry? Far older than either of us might guess, probably. Yet here, right before our eyes, the beginning of the end is shaping up. Kentipoos and his people won't go without a struggle. They'll fight like demons — but hopelessly. The fact scares me and in no way bolsters my faith in humanity."

The sternness in Henry Gallatin's face deepened.

"Thinking the same way, I've found that a man can do himself out of all peace of mind. So now I look at the sky and feel of the earth and find my comfort in knowing they'll always be there, no matter what else may happen."

Vinegar Spring lay some seven miles north and west of the Gallatin headquarters. Computing time and distance, Sebastian turned away.

"Be back to spend the night with you, Henry."

At the waiting pack string he found Sam Lester scowling.

"Ward, you notice them fellers who just rode in?"

Sebastian shook his head. "What about them?"

"Ten or a dozen in the bunch. More of them so-called civilian volunteers who just ain't happy unless they're out trying to shoot themselves another poor squaw or some old warrior plumb past his fighting age. Same damned breed as was in on that Desolation Flat affair." Sam spat his disgust.

"Know any of them?" asked Sebastian.

"One. Yance McCloud."

Sebastian considered this soberly, lips tightening. He shrugged.

"I'm sorry for Kitty's sake, but Yance will find his own way to hell."

By the time they reached Vinegar Spring, turned their pack loads over to Bill Wiggin and his helper, rested their string while they put together and ate a meal, afternoon was fading into a gray, chill shroud. Heading back for the Gallatin ranch they were met by a few spits of snow, and the cold deepened steadily until the earth, half frozen, rang under the hoof of horse and mule.

Out in the darkening east the chemistry of icy air, touching slightly warmer water, spawned a mist above Tule Lake. Rising and thickening, this pushed out on all sides, washing like a tide across the tule flats and boggy meadows, to pile up against the low lift of the lava rims, then flow over them and beyond.

So the world became drowned in a dank and freezing fog, and men moving through it found it beading brow and eyelash with icy drops and chilling their cheeks to numbness. At the military camp at the Gallatin ranch, watch fires dwindled to a dull and near-smothered glow. Sound grew muffled, and as night deepened, all movement and sound faded out until the world seemed an inert, dead thing. In their blankets, soldiers facing their first hostile engagement, both officers and enlisted men alike, slept fitfully, restlessly. Of these, Lieutenant Philip Ashland was one.

In his command tent, Colonel Frank Wheaton slept not at all, just lay staring wide-eyed into the icy darkness, haunted with responsibility.

Dawn. January 17, 1873. Dawn, frozen and bitter. Bugles shrilling, sounding thin and drained through the smother of fog. Campfires coming sluggishly to life. Men crowding close about the reluctant flames, gulping coffee, eating meager rations. Excitement gradually growing, getting into their blood, warming them and stirring some to swaggering brag.

Henry Gallatin, muffled to the eyes in a long, blanketlined coat, moved about in the vague morning light, taking care of what few chores he could under the handicap of the military tangle all about him. He heard some of the brags and knew a mingling of anger and irritation — and some slight pity.

"Come noon," a civilian volunteer was boasting, "the fightin' will be done with and we'll be back here, sittin' up proper to our grub. Me, I'm hopin' the damned Modocs just last long enough for me to get my good share of them."

Henry Gallatin turned on him, stern eyes flashing.

"You are a great and mouthy fool, and of a breed I do not care for. A soldier's honorable job is to fight, whether the issue be just or otherwise, for such is not of his making. But you and your kind will not leave him alone to it, but must edge in like damned ghouls, eager to be in on the slaughter. Yet this thing will not be as easy as you say. Take care you're not curled up in hell, long before noon!"

Ward Sebastian and Sam Lester were caring for their pack string when Sam came face to face with a burly trooper wearing sergeant's chevrons. Sam stopped him.

"Remember me, soldier? I was with the pack string that got tangled in your camp back in Shasta Valley. I told you then you were going up against a tough chore. Better believe it."

Grimes, the sergeant, nodded soberly. "I'd never seen any of this lava country before. Now that I have, I'm thinking you may be right, friend."

Sam dropped a hand on the sergeant's arm. "Good luck, soldier!"

The bugles shrilled again, quickening their demanding cadence. Faintly distant to the east, almost like

164

ghost voices, came answering calls. Out there a further detachment of the First Cavalry, unable to maneuver as cavalry in the broken lava, would advance on foot. The attack theory was to strike the stronghold of Kentipoos and his people from east and west simultaneously and so crush all opposition in this pincers movement.

It was a good theory. Only, there was the lava, and the fierce occupants of it.

Early morning, January 17, 1873.

The attack finally getting under way. Men advancing up to the lava plain, then on across it, rifles at ready and eyes straining into the fog.

Ordinarily, Ward Sebastian and Sam Lester would have been long gone from the Gallatin ranch, would had their outfit on the trail by the first touch of daylight. But this was a day holding a harsh and momentous fascination, and Sebastian found he could not ride away from it. Along with Henry Gallatin and Sam Lester he listened to the shrilling bugles and watched the troops take formation and move off into the wet curtain of the fog.

Sam Lester stirred restlessly, scowling.

"I've cussed them more than once. The military, I mean. Then I see them moving out like now and somehow the feeling gets me that I ought to be going with them, even though they're headin' into a ruckus I don't believe in at all, and are set to shoot down some poor Modoc devils I figger got as much right to live as we have. How's a man to square himself with himself, when his feelings keep naggin' him this way and that?"

Sebastian replied soberly. "It's the tie of blood telling a man one thing, while his heart tells him another, and his head trying to find a fair and happy balance somewhere in between. But no man can be all things to all people, Sam."

"That's right," Henry Gallatin agreed. "I've plenty of sympathy for the Modocs, as you well know. But I feel sorry for them soldiers too. Lot of them ain't much more than boys, who got little idea what they're heading into." He paused to shake his head regretfully. "A lot of them won't ever come out of the lavas, and them that do won't ever be the same again. They'll be older, their youth all burned up, all gone."

Major Ross Ashland came hurrying through the mist, nodding to Sebastian and Sam, but putting his words at Henry Gallatin.

"Colonel Wheaton's compliments, Mr. Gallatin. The colonel anticipates a considerable number of wounded and foresees the need of your ranch house as a temporary hospital. May we count on that?"

"Of course," said Henry Gallatin quietly. "I'll help you get things in shape."

"Major," asked Sebastian, "where's Phil?"

The major jerked an uneasy head toward the lava plain.

"Out there somewhere, leading his platoon. Wish I could trade places with him for I promised Connie faithfully I'd look after him. Yet, any soldier has to take his chances, and I can only wish the boy luck and hope he handles himself well."

166

"That," Sebastian said, "I'm sure he'll do. And Major, Sam and I are feeling mighty useless about now. Is there any way we can help?"

"Not from the shooting end," said Major Ashland bluntly. "Nothing personal, you understand, but I don't believe in this civilian volunteer business. Fighting is the Army's business, and the Army is here. On the other hand, if the pair of you would care to man a stretcher and carry some poor wounded devil out of the lavas — ?"

"Consider it done," Sebastian said.

Out on the lava plain, Lieutenant Phil Ashland was going into his first action in as sound a frame of mind as could be expected of one of his age and temperament. Of military family, there never had been any doubt that the service would be his career, and his was the deep, quiet pride of the professional soldier.

Last night, before seeking his blankets he had written two letters by lantern light, and left them where they must be found if his personal gear was gone over. One was to his sister, Connie. The other, a much longer one, was to Kitty Dutra. Thinking on these now, put his mind at rest. All else was up to the god of battles.

So up to the lavas and into them they went, in a long skirmish line, under the wet shroud of a fog that seemed to increase in density with every step, and over terrain growing ever rougher and wilder. A ghost world, through which men moved like phantoms, in a line which became more and more ragged, bulging ahead here, sagging back there, as the savage plain shaped the movement of these men to its own contours.

Almost immediately the lava began showing its fangs. Flinty spines, hidden in stunted sagebrush, caught at unwary feet and sent men sprawling. Pot holes yawned suddenly where footing had been solid a stride or two before. Crevices, masked and treacherous, waited like the open jaws of some sinister trap, and in one of these a trooper found his battle ended before a single shot was fired. The crevice tripped him, and with his foot still locked in the jaws of lava, his leg snapped cleanly as he fell. His cry of pain was but the first of the voiced agonies to come.

Ever the way grew more torturous. Men, their progress limited to what they could edge around, or crawl or climb over, began losing contact with fellow troopers on either hand, and so found themselves alone in the fog, fearfully alone.

Came the first gunshot, sounding hollow and unreal off to the left of Lieutenant Phil Ashland and the men of his platoon. But it was real enough, for over there a lanky, hatchet-faced civilian volunteer whom Henry Gallatin had warned to beware of hell, crumpled down, a bright froth of crimson bubbling at his lips as he coughed his life away.

The gun that killed him had flared pale in the fog not five yards in front of him, and neither he, before he died, nor any other of his group, saw anything of the cunningly hidden Modoc warrior who had done for him.

That single shot seemed a signal for others. There was no concerted volley fire, just a rippling of reports scattered through the fog, some round and solid and close at hand, others muffled and faint with distance.

All along that stumbling, wavering skirmish line, men began going down, some silently, slugged to instant oblivion by a deadly bullet delivered at point-blank range. Others, wounded, set up their thin crying for aid.

A gun flared in the fog, the report blasting — so it seemed to Phil Ashland — almost in his face. But it was a trooper, pushing up beside him through the gray-white froth of the mists who grunted under heavy impact, spun around and fell spread-eagled, flat on his back, his dead eyes staring up in a faintly bewildered astonishment.

Shaken, Phil threw an answering shot with his revolver, but had no idea where or what he hit, if anything. He turned to shout an order to his men, found none of them in sight. He yelled, ordering them to reply, to keep contact. There was no answer. Except for the dead trooper lying at his feet, he was completely alone, the dank mists swirling about him, his sense of direction faulty and uncertain.

He fought back a faint thread of panic, orienting himself by the increasing sound of battle, by the thumping cacophony of the guns; guns out ahead and to either side of him, as troopers began shooting back at those mocking, deadly muzzle flashes, seeing nothing more substantial for a target. Then also, there were the bugles, blasting their fog-muffled brassiness from both east and west, now reflecting a worried, uncertain urgency.

On the heels of a particularly smothered, blunted gun report not far from Phil, a man cried and cried again in wild agony, then went abruptly silent. Right after, there was a sudden floundering of approach and a trooper came lunging through a thicket of cherry brush. At sight of Phil he reared to a stop, jamming his rifle forward. The muzzle of the weapon was scarcely a foot from Phil's face, and he knocked it aside with a desperately warding arm barely before it blasted flame and report.

The licking flame, the smash of report so close to his head, staggered Phil Ashland. When he recovered and caught his balance he tongue-whipped the trooper savagely, recognizing him as one of his own. It had been a very near thing and the trooper was abject in his apologies.

"God's witness, Leftenant sir, I had no idea. This damned fog — them — them Modocs! They just killed Jess Parker. We were hunkered down, Jess and me. We were lost. We were tryin' to figger where the rest of the boys were, so we could join 'em. This fog, sir! Then this gun goes off, almost right under us, seemed to me. The slug plumb lifted Jess, then dropped him. He hollered — God, how he hollered! I never heard a man holler that way before in my life. Then, jest as quick, he wasn't hollering no more. Old Jess was dead —!"

Recalling the dread moment, his terror coming back, the trooper was wild again and plainly ready to bolt. Phil caught hold of him, swung him around and hit him hard across the shoulders with a clenched fist, giving harsh order.

"None of that, none of that! Get hold of yourself. Stick close to me!"

With the voicing of the order, steadiness came back to Lieutenant Phil Ashland. A coolness he had not known since the attack began, coursed through him. It was like a runner catching his second wind. He began to reason calmly. Before becoming separated from him, the body of his platoon had been to his right, so he began angling that way, all his senses reaching and straining. Half a stride behind him came the trooper, clumsy footed, still mumbling his fear to himself.

Far out in the clammy, dripping mystery ahead, guns were now hammering an almost solid echo, and here and there around Phil, small scattered impacts sounded. At first he did not understand, but when one of the impacts was followed by the sullen, fading whimper of a ricochet, he had his answer. These were spent bullets from the guns of the dismounted cavalry, fighting in from the east.

Grimly, Phil thought, we could kill them, or they us, in this fog.

Now again, on the heels of another of the close in, strangely smothered gun reports, lifted the high, agonized crying of a mortally stricken man. At the sound, the trooper with Phil whined like a frightened animal and charged blindly off, boots scraping and crunching on lava rock, brush crackling under his lunging weight. He ran right out into a second of silence, followed instantly by a wail of stark terror, the more heart-stopping because of the manner in which it tailed off swiftly into a muffled, downward-fading note

171

into the depths of the earth itself. It ceased abruptly when, from far below, lifted the sound of sodden impact.

Spine prickling, Phil Ashland followed where the trooper had gone, moving ahead with the greatest care. Instinct, as much as anything, stopped him short of a scanty fringe of brush. Beyond that brush fringe lay an irregular, yawning blackness some ten or twelve feet across. Carrying up out of that Stygian pit came the small, faint echo of trickling lava fragments, striking solidly down there.

Cold to the core, Phil backed away. Now, off to his right, he heard voices and when he moved that way, found men of his strayed platoon, hunkered down behind a low rim. Grimes, the burly sergeant, swore his relief.

"Seeing you safe, puts heart in me again, Lieutenant. This is pure hell. The men went to make a fight of it, if they could just see something to fight. So far, there's been nothing but gun flashes. And after every one, it seems, there's another man down, dead or wounded. I tell you this lava is hell, full of hidden devils!"

Phil nodded, dropping to his heels. "Where are the rest of the men?"

"Scanson and Murray both dead, sir. Barrow and Dean back yonder a bit, wounded. Barrow's bad, good as dead I'm afraid. Some of the others got scattered. Like Parker and French. I ain't see either of them since we got into these damned lavas."

"They're both done for." Phil's words ran a little tight. "Parker was shot. French was with me for a little

172

time but he stampeded and ran right into a pot hole that dropped him only God knows how far."

"You mean — buried alive, sir?"

"He fell too far to stay alive."

Of a sudden, Phil was avid with thirst, his lips parched, his tongue a file across them. Grimes pushed a canteen at him and he held himself to a single mouthful, his pride keeping him steady in the matter. He stood up, straightening his shoulders.

"All right, men! We go ahead. Keep within a stride of one another if you can, so there'll be no more scattering. Guide on me."

So they went ahead, slowly, carefully, but ahead. Over the merciless lava. It sliced at the soles of their boots. It scraped and gouged and brought blood wherever it touched when a man stumbled or fell. It threw up ragged spines and flinty rims to bar their way and challenge them. It opened in yawning, black-mawed pits which they had to carefully circle, while the bitter phlegm of stark fear thickened their throats. It fought them every step of the way, the lava did. The damned, malignant lava . . .

The fog refused to lift or thin, and for all they knew by visual judgment, they were alone in it. Phil Ashland, as well as his men, had this feeling. He knew better, of course. Other men were out there somewhere, hundreds of them. The ragged persistence of rifle fire told this, as did the occasional shouts, some close, some far off.

Then there was the fog-blunted tenor song of the bugles, which now served to confuse, rather than help.

All told of men at grips with a hostile terrain, but unable to get at an elusive, deadly enemy who, cunningly using the trickery of a tangled hell of lava and the stealthy shroud of the fog, killed and killed again, without loss to himself.

The Modoc, well aware that here was the beginning of the end for him and all his people, knowing that there neither could or would be any drawing back and that eternity waited his ancient heritage, fought with every deadly trick he knew. He used one now.

Some among him could speak the white man's language, and a voice called through the smother.

"Over here, you men — over here!"

The words were plain, but the tone was guttural, and an alarm rang in Lieutenant Phil Ashland's brain and he held his men back. But some stray troopers, lost to their command and desperate to make contact again, closed in on the call. Rifle fire burst from the lava all about them, and there they died, four of them.

The casualty list grew steadily. The dead lay in many places, twisted by their brief agonies. Among the wounded some stoically contained their sufferings and some groaned and cursed. Some cried their fear and pain aloud, while others lay still and silent, dying and aware of it. The able-bodied did what they could for their less fortunate comrades.

The day dragged on and the painful yard-by-yard advance slowed and came to a complete halt, the frustration of the attackers growing until it became absolute. Officers urged, ordered, exhorted, cursed — to no end. Troopers turned sullen, feeling that their

174

own little group, already rent and thinned by death and wounds, was all that was left to carry on hopelessly.

So now all cohesion of forces had been lost, and direct line of command no longer existed. And when distant bugles shouted brassily, men no longer cared or listened. The virus of complete defeat was there and steadily deepening. Men began to skulk and slither away, intent on but one thing — to find a way out of this deadly trap of fog-shrouded lava where death struck suddenly and mercilessly and unseen.

In this first small, ebbing movement the retreat began, beyond all will of the high command to stop. It quickened until verging on outright rout. Phil Ashland tried to hold the remnants of his little command together, but in the space of less than a minute, lost another man killed and another man wounded. And it was while he and Grimes, his faithful sergeant, were caring for this wounded one that the distant, nervous bugles finally sounded a note which men would now pay attention to. It was recall.

The sound was as welcome to Phil Ashland as to his men. Vaguely he wondered if he shouldn't know shame at his feeling of relief, for recall in this battle spelled defeat — defeat in the first real action of his military career. Perhaps, according to the shouters and flag wavers, he should have known shame. But he didn't. Instead, just a vast relief.

Relief, and now a strange, straining weakness, for with the purpose of the attack gone, there came the exhaustion of nerves worn and shredded by strain and tension. And also the sudden, ravening battle hunger began its gnawing in his belly. He weaved a trifle on his feet.

Except for Grimes, the sergeant, Phil's men began moving off without waiting his order. He shouted at them, reminding them of their lately wounded comrade. At his elbow, Grimes said:

"No need, sir. Moore is gone."

Phil dropped on one knee beside the lately wounded one.

"Moore —?"

There was no answer. There never would be again from the sprawled trooper.

Phil pulled slowly erect. His men had already vanished in the fog. He began to curse them, a little brokenly. Grimes touched his arm.

"Steady, sir. Considering everything, you can't rightly blame them. A man can't fight what he can't see or make contact with."

Phil nodded, quieting. "Let's get out of here."

It wasn't easy, getting out. The lavas were still there and the wily Modoc had got in behind the advance and now harried retreat with more of that murderous, close-range fire from rim and pot hole and hidden covert. So men died in retreat as they had in advance, and blind terror began having its way with the survivors. They tore clothing and skin to bloody rags in their wild fight to get clear of the clutch of the lava.

As he and Sergeant Grimes made their way along, a fuller measure of strength returned to Phil Ashland, which he needed. For the same fringes and thickets of stubborn brush were there to fight through, the same yawning pot holes and crevices to be warily circled and crossed, the same spines and tortuous rims to be painfully climbed over.

Abruptly there was a crouched, darting shadow, whisking from one pocket of lava to another. Sergeant Grimes called sharp warning to Phil. With the warning a gun flared, opening a pale bloom in the fog.

Two blows, two impacts, struck Phil Ashland. One in the chest, massively. Then a lesser, duller one against his back and shoulders as he fell before the power of the Modoc bullet and the lava leaped to meet him.

Instantly, all things became dim and far away. The reports of two more gunshots, though close to him, reached his ears as lost and fading echoes. He knew no pain, only a great lightness of feeling that carried him away to a world of nothingness.

Sergeant Grimes, driving a quick shot at the flitting, malignant shadow, had seen it falter slightly. Yet, tenacious as a wounded panther, it twisted and slithered behind a sheltering outcrop, and from there threw another slug from the Henry rifle it carried, a slug which tore its lethal way through the staunch heart of Sergeant Asa Grimes.

Pain. Pain and thirst. These were the things that brought a degree of consciousness back to Lieutenant Phil Ashland. The pain filled his chest, a sodden, deathly feeling. But it was the thirst that was the worse, the more insistent. It was a raging fire all through him. And it was not the pain, but the frantic need for water which forced its way past his lips until he cried it aloud. Weakly, but aloud.

And then the neck of a canteen was against his feverish lips, and the wet, wonderful caress of water across his swollen tongue and down his throat. But so little of it! Just two short swallows, when a gallon would not have been enough. He would have fought for that canteen, had he known any strength.

But the hands that had tendered it, now took it away, and a gruff, tired voice spoke.

"Easy does it, soldier. We got to make this stuff last. Easy does it!"

CHAPTER
TWELVE

Riding in one of the ambulance wagons which maneuvered a way as deeply into the lava plain as possible, Ward Sebastian and Sam Lester met the first backwash of the battle, the walking wounded. They came slowly, faces drained, eyes dull and staring from shock. There was a lot of them and ambulance wagons, quickly filling, went rocking and creaking away.

Sebastian and Sam, laden with canteens and stretcher, worked into the lava, searching. Far out ahead, rifle fire was a distant spatter of dull echoes, marking the line of advance.

The universal cry for water led them to the wounded they were seeking. It was rough, punishing work. To move surely through the lavas unencumbered, was difficult enough. To carry one end of a loaded stretcher through the same country was far worse. Yet it wasn't merely the physical end of it which was demanding and exhausting; more so did the agony of these soldiers, so many of them so young, lay as a weight across a man's mind and sympathy.

They lost count of time and grew numbed and dulled by their own weariness. Twice they emerged from the lavas, only to find that the trooper they had carried out had died on the stretcher. After which there was nothing to do but lay the dead man aside and go back in search of a living one.

They were deep in the lavas when the bugles shrilled recall, but that meant nothing to them even when retreating troopers burst through the fog, stumbling and hurrying. Sebastian and Sam saw the fear and the defeat in the faces of these men and, remembering the dead they had come across, wondered at the uselessness of it all.

They worked their way past another of the interminable flinty outcrops and saw three figures down in an area of a few short yards. Two were in Army blue, the third a volunteer in civilian clothes, this one half lying, half sitting, propped against a spine of lava, his head sagging. Just beyond him lay one of the blue-clad figures. On this side of him sprawled the other, and Sam Lester, looking down, swore softly.

"It's that sergeant, Ward — Sergeant Grimes. Just this mornin' I was talking to him. Now —!" Sam shook his head sadly. "He was a good feller. I liked him."

At the sound of Sam's voice the civilian volunteer stirred and lifted his head, showing a face gone gray and cut deep with lines of suffering. It was Yance McCloud. He spoke warning, his voice weak and slow.

"Watch yourselves! A wounded Modoc just yonder. I saw him once, heard him move a couple of times. Maybe he's dead — by now. Maybe he's just waitin' to get himself another — whole man. Watch him!"

Even as Yance finished speaking, Ward Sebastian heard the faint ring of gun metal slithering over lava rock. He came around fast, reaching for the gun at his hip. A dozen times this day, toiling with his end of the loaded stretcher, he had cursed the weight of the weapon, had even thought of laying it aside. Now, however, as he drew and leveled it, he blessed the solid, lethal heft of it.

Dim through the fog the shadowy outline of a shaggy head and pair of shoulders lifted above the edge of a close-by lava pocket. Sebastian drove a swift, point-blank shot. The figure sagged and slid from sight again, the rifle it was leveling, clattering loosely on the lava.

Gun poised for another shot if necessary, Sebastian moved over to the pocket and had his look. When he returned, Sam Lester asked thinly:

"Know that one?"

Sebastian nodded. "Chumlucky Pete," he said harshly. "When he worked for me he was faithful and harmless. Now — !" He bent over Yance McCloud. "How bad are you hurt, Yance?"

"Too bad," came the answer in a tired, resigned voice. "Don't bother with me. See what you can do for this young officer beside me."

Sebastian stepped past Yance and knelt beside the figure in blue. He called sharply.

"Give a hand here, Sam. It's Phil Ashland!"

It was a white, drained face he looked down into, an unconscious face, with the stain of blood at one lip corner, and Sebastian's first thought was that Phil was surely dead. Then he saw the flutter of breathing stir the blood-crusted front of Phil's tunic.

"Sam!" he called again.

Between them they lifted and eased the limp, slack figure on to their stretcher, after which Sebastian opened the tunic and had a look at the wound. The bullet had gone completely through the right side of Phil Ashland's chest.

"Bad," muttered Sebastian grimly. "That bullet went through a lung. But as long as it didn't stop inside, maybe he has a chance. We'll cushion him all we can. The sergeant yonder will never need his tunic and shirt again. Get them, Sam."

While they worked, Yance McCloud began to talk.

"I was farther back when I got mine. In the belly. Knew right away I was done for. Just a matter of time when you get it — down there. But I didn't figger to wait around until the squaws found me and went to work on me. Not that I'd blame them any, of course — not after the things I've helped do to them."

Sebastian threw a swift glance at Yance. Here was something he'd never expected to hear from this man. Yance went on.

"I figgered to get clear of the lavas if I could. I heard somebody callin' for water. I took a look and saw — him. I had a little left in my canteen, and gave it to him. Which reminds me. Right now — I could use a drink myself —"

A note of desperate, feverish need had built up in Yance McCloud's voice, and when Sebastian proffered a canteen, Yance's gripping hands shook so he could barely lift the container to his avid lips. He put it aside presently and sighed deeply. Just a ghost of a smile touched him, and now his voice took on a thin, far away shading.

"Heard a sawbones say one time never to give water to a man with a bullet in his belly. That feller never had one in his or knew what real thirst is."

Yance lifted the canteen and took another drink.

While Yance had talked on in that shadowy, far-away voice, Sebastian and Sam had been getting Phil Ashland ready to move. They had cushioned the stretcher with the folded shirt and tunic of the dead sergeant. Sebastian turned to Yance McCloud again and found Yance's eyes steadily on him, and something in the look gave Sebastian pause. His voice went gruff.

"We'll be back after you, Yance."

Yance shook his head. "Be a useless trip. By then I won't be around any more. You might leave the canteen; still some comfort in it for me. You'll be — seeing Kitty, maybe?"

"Expect to."

"Tell her I said good-by — and good luck. Tell her it took a Modoc bullet through my belly to make me realize how damned useless I've been. Tell her I gave another man water — that I wanted awful bad myself. Tell her I think I died a better man than I lived. You'll do that, Ward?"

"All of it, Yance. Here's the canteen — and my hand."

Yance McCloud smiled again, and past the lines of suffering his face reflected a quietness, the serenity of a man now at peace with himself. His voice dropped to a wondering murmur.

"Somehow, this makes things right. Yet it's a hell of a note when a man has to die to find out what he might have lived for. There's a joke in this somewhere — a joke on me!"

Major Kress was burly, red-faced and reeked of whisky. His bared arms and surgeon's apron were smeared with the carmine of men's blood. Straightening from his examination of the still figure on the stretcher beside the Gallatin ranch-house door, he shook his head, his voice a blunt growl.

"Very little chance. Under the best of conditions, maybe. As they are, no. A bullet-punctured lung is very bad at any time. Here it's wicked, for this cursed freezing fog is enough to give a sound man congestion of the lungs. The fever is already working in this boy. Wish I could say something different, Ashland, but there it is."

Major Ashland's face was desperate.

"You're full of whisky, Kress — in no condition to judge. You should be reported!"

"Of course I got whisky in me," came the curt retort. "And until this nightmare is over with I'll keep on having it in me. But never too much to keep me from knowing exactly what I'm doing — and doing it right! You should trade places with me, Ashland, and meet the look of some poor devil whose shattered arm or leg has to come off, and who knows it. You'd find yourself reaching for the whisky bottle too. But damn it, man, as a senior professional officer and soldier, you should be able to face facts!"

Major Kress turned to go back into the ranch house, a place filled with wounded men and with the plaint of their agony. He paused, and his voice came across his shoulder, quiet and tired.

"I don't blame you, Ashland. That boy is your nephew, isn't he? Well, sometimes I feel that stating a casualty has no chance, is arrogance in the face of God. Now if you could get the boy quickly into a good bed where you could keep him warm and still and nurse him closely every minute of the day and night — and remember to pray — yes, especially remember to pray — then he might, I'm saying he barely might, pull through. But with what we can do for him here, never!"

Major Kress drew a deep breath as though bracing himself for further effort, then went inside.

Major Ross Ashland turned to Ward Sebastian, shoulders sagging.

"He's right, of course. And he's really a very able man. I had no right to say what I did to him. But I — Phil —"

He shook his head, brushing a hand across his eyes.

"Major," Sebastian said, "Phil isn't dead yet, and until he is I'm not believing he's going to die. Kress said if we could get him to a place where he'd be sheltered and nursed properly, he'd have a chance. That place is my ranch. With your permission, Sam and I will take him there."

"That's miles away," Major Ashland said dully. "And the road a rough hell. He'd never make it."

"We got to make the try," insisted Sebastian. "We won't move him in a wagon. We'll carry him on a

185

tarpaulin slung between two mules. Sam and I brought a woman over forty miles that way one time to the doctor in Yreka. She lived, and so did her baby. This is Phil's only chance. Do we take it?"

Major Ashland straightened, spoke quietly.

"Of course. And thanks for thinking clearly, while I've been fuzzy headed. How can I help?"

"Blankets, several of them. Sam, we'll take the same pair of mules we used to carry Mrs. Trent that time. We'll come back for the rest of the string later. Let's hustle this!"

They slung the heavy canvas tarpaulin between the two mules and padded it deep with blankets. They wrapped Phil Ashland in still more blankets, lifted him into place and made more lashings to secure him there.

"He'll ride like a baby in that sling," Sebastian said. "And with the mules giving off their animal heat on each side of him, he'll be warm. All right, Sam, we travel!"

"I'll be furnishing some of the prayers Kress advised," Major Ashland said huskily. "And once it is sure, either way, I'd appreciate the word."

The afternoon was a good half gone, with the promise of another bleak and freezing night ahead. And as the Gallatin ranch and all that it held faded into the chill murk, the feeling came to Ward Sebastian that he'd just emerged from a nightmare of unreality.

Here were no sounding guns, no bugles tenoring their high, nervous calls. Here no wounded thinly crying, no dead men lying crouched and twisted. Here was complete and soothing silence, broken only by the

186

thump of hoofs on earth and the occasional small creak of saddle leather.

Round about was the kind of world he'd known all his years. This was the season of its sternness, but its gentler moods were well remembered and would come again. By that time, perhaps, men would have learned how to live together . . .

They kept the mules to as fast a pace as possible under conditions, but the leaden daylight had faded out and a good hour of Stygian darkness ridden through before they crossed the final rim and in the far-running basin beyond, picked up the faint glitter of the ranch lights.

Old Bob Gayle heard them coming in and was there to challenge them, and when reassured by Sam Lester's reply, exclaimed with mild profanity.

"What the hell! Where's the rest of the string?"

"Back at Henry Gallatin's," Sebastian told him. "Get a lantern going. We've a wounded man here, Bob."

In the scant spray of the lantern light they lifted Phil Ashland carefully to the ground. Sebastian put a hand inside the cocoon of blankets He straightened with a relieved, tired sigh.

"Still with us, Sam. I felt him stir a little. But he's on fire with fever. I'll go prepare the womenfolks."

The three women were gathered around the kitchen table. When Sebastian stepped through the door, tall and shadowy out of the night, it was Connie Ashland who came to her feet, warm gladness on her lips.

"Ward!"

He came up to the table and as the fuller light touched him, something in his expression put her hand at her throat.

"Ward — what's wrong? Phil — Uncle Ross —?"

"Phil," he said steadily. "Wounded. Sam Lester and I brought him here for care and nursing."

"Phil — wounded!" Now it was Kitty Dutra on her feet, facing Sebastian, catching him by both arms, her voice going husky with dread. "The truth, Ward! How — how bad?"

He was startled at what he saw in Kitty's eyes, for he had not guessed anything like this. Understanding turned his words gentle.

"Bad enough. The Army doctor said he'd need prayer as well as the best of nursing to pull him through." He looked at Connie again. "He's a very sick boy. I know you wouldn't want me to tell it wrong."

She showed him the full measure of her courage. Her face was pale and drained, but her voice held quite steady.

"The room I've been using. Bring him there."

So they carried Phil in, stripped away the blood-stained uniform, put him to bed. No fresh bleeding showed, but the young soldier's cheeks were hectic with livid color, and he was beginning to mumble strange incoherencies.

"It's the fever," Mrs. Gayle said grimly, "that's the mean devil we must whip. If we don't, it will burn him up."

188

A sick man coughed and kept on coughing. Weakly, but with a persistent, wet thickness that was queerly frightening. A small sound, yet one which carried all through the ranch house, despite stout walls and closed doors. Day and night now for a full week it had been going on, and only by leaving the house completely could you get away from it.

But Ward Sebastian never stayed away long. For, he told himself, if three women could stand up to the ever-deepening threat, of which the cough was the dread voice, then certainly he could. So he sent Sam Lester and Bob Gayle back to the Gallatin ranch after the pack string, while he stayed on here to give all help he could.

It was as Mrs. Gayle had said. The fever was the thing, even more malignant than the bullet wound that had occasioned it. So they fought it without rest or letup, and with every recourse they knew. And they watched Phil Ashland go far, far away from them, until they held him by the barest thread.

Mrs. Gayle was solid, methodical, determined, but her years began to limit her activity, so it was Connie Ashland and Kitty Dutra who stood the brunt of it. They were ever at Phil's bedside, fighting — yielding not an inch. They hardly ate, and if they slept at all, it was a short, fitful moment of dozing. They grew haggard and worn, but in the depths of their eyes, one pair gray, the other dark, an unquenchable spark flamed and held. Between the pair of them they placed their hands on Phil Ashland and held the life in him.

Occasionally the almost unbearable strain would wring tears from Kitty Dutra, and Connie would comfort her. Only once did Connie show the need of being comforted herself.

Sebastian had just brought in another armful of wood, fuel for fires never allowed to go out. Connie Ashland came into the kitchen after another pan of water for the sick room. Sebastian stood silently, watching her, wishing there was something more he could do to aid this gallant girl in this rough hour.

She seemed to read his thought, for abruptly she put the pan down, turned and walked straight into his arms, clinging to him, pressing her face against him, while a short spasm of dry sobbing racked her. He held her tightly, saying nothing until she quieted and pulled away from him.

"You've got to rest," he told her gently. "You and Kitty both go get a good sleep. I'll keep sick watch."

"No." Her tone was set. "No. If we slept now, we'd lose him. He needs us every second."

Sebastian did not argue the point. While another winter's night deepened in chill outside, he sat there with them, beside a man whose soul hung at the brink.

Hours later he went out for more wood for the hearth fire. On re-entering the house he was instantly aware of a change, over which he puzzled tiredly. Then he understood. The cough no longer sounded.

He hurried to the sick room. On their knees beside the bed were Connie Ashland and Kitty Dutra, arms about each other, their common sobbing the only sound.

Sebastian stood silently, feeling all empty and raw and let down inside. So it was done with. The good fight lost, and in this case at least, the power of faith flouted and useless. Well, he concluded bleakly, it had been hopeless from the first.

He dropped a hand on Connie Ashland's shoulder.

"They don't come any braver than you two. I only wish —"

He broke off, startled at what he saw in her transfigured face as she lifted her head and looked up at him. The haggard weariness was gone and behind her tears was a new vitality, a glowing look of triumph.

"We've won, Ward!" she cried softly. "We've won!"

Sebastian looked past her then, at the figure on the bed. No dead man, this, but one with the savage fever fire fading from the drawn face, replaced by the shine of sweat.

And in some strange way, substance had returned to Phil Ashland.

CHAPTER
THIRTEEN

Despite their relief and renewed hopes, all at the ranch knew that Phil Ashland was still a very sick boy, and that any kind of reverse or complication would almost certainly prove fatal. So the schedule of faithful nursing did not slacken.

Sam Lester brought the pack string back from Gallatin's, but Sebastian, though restless for the freedom and action and pressing business of the trail again, stayed close to the ranch for the better part of three weeks until sure that Phil was certain of full recovery. Then, true to his promise, he made the ride to the Gallatin ranch and sought out Major Ross Ashland.

On getting the word, Major Ashland turned away for a moment while he cleared his throat and blew his nose. Then he came around and spoke gruffly.

"Almost more than I could have hoped for. You really do feel the boy is going to make it?"

"Sure of it, Major. After watching Connie and Kitty Dutra hold onto him and bring him back out of nowhere, I can see no chance of them letting go of him, now. Those two have been wonderful."

"They would be, of course," nodded the major. "Yet the boy is alive today mainly because of what you did.

You brought him in out of the lavas and then carried him safely to your ranch. Which surely saved him, not only for the reasons Major Kress first gave, but for another he could not foresee at the time. Because a few days after the battle, some kind of damned epizootic hit among the wounded here — an influenza, Kress called it. Whatever it was, it took off a lot of the more seriously wounded. It was very bad."

"Bound to be. And there's more to come, Major."

"Afraid so," Major Ashland agreed. "Unless General Canby can set up some kind of peaceful settlement."

"General Canby! That's going high, isn't it?"

Major Ashland shrugged.

"Quite. Latest theory out of Washington. Canby is on his way in. Meanwhile, Colonel Gillem of the First Cavalry has taken over active command from Colonel Wheaton. I feel sorry for Frank Wheaton. It wasn't his idea to attempt to dig the Modocs out of that lava stronghold, though I suppose he'll be blamed because things didn't go according to plan. I doubt anyone could have done better. The lava, the fog — it all contributed."

"It was rough," Sebastian said.

"Rough! A mild word. Hell is better. For that is the kind of whipping we took, Ward — a very hell of a whipping! Most of our men never saw a Modoc, much less have the chance to take real offensive action. If we have to go back into those lavas again, I hate to think of the men we'll lose. Let's hope Canby brings the answer."

"He won't," said Sebastian flatly. "It's too late now for any chance at peace."

Major Ashland regarded him soberly. "But Kentipoos must know that he and his people haven't a chance over the long haul?"

"Certainly he knows it. But he and his people have been lied to and deceived too often by we whites to ever believe any promise of ours again, no matter who brings it, whether it be General Canby or President Grant, for that matter."

"You make it sound pretty hopeless."

"That is the way I see it. I know the Modocs pretty well, Major. They've been pushed and hounded too far for any return. They've called on their ancient gods and made ancient medicine. They've sung their death song and are not afraid to go. But before they do, they'll take all the whites they can with them."

An orderly came, with summons from Colonel Gillem for Major Ashland, who shook hands with Sebastian.

"Thanks again, Ward — for bringing me the word. You may guess at my relief and thanksgiving. Give my best to Connie. Tell her I'm proud of her and that I'll be along to see her and Phil as soon as I can wangle a day away from duty. Take care of yourself."

Major Ashland hurried off and then, as Sebastian turned to his horse, it was Captain Judson Dillon who came up to him. As usual, Dillon's manner was curt and faintly edged with arrogance. He showed Sebastian the briefest of nods.

"You bring word of Phil Ashland?"

194

"That's right."

"He is — still alive?"

"And going to stay so." Sebastian went into his saddle.

"When can he be moved?" Dillon asked.

Sebastian got out his pipe, began packing it. "Why think of that? There's no rush. Let's just be thankful that he pulled through."

"That goes without saying," Dillon said stiffly.

"Then why the concern about moving him?"

"You're forgetting something, Sebastian. Sick or well, alive or dead, Phil Ashland belongs to the Army, subject to its care and decision."

Sebastian spoke dryly.

"The last official Army decision I recall concerning Phil Ashland was that he was sure to die, which was that! And I'm not holding the decision against the Army, either, for in the light of conditions as they were at the moment, it seemed entirely justified. The point is, however, that after the Army had given him up, some of us ordinary civilians, didn't.

"The Army didn't save Phil Ashland's life, Captain. Three devoted women at my ranch did. His sister Constance, Kitty Dutra and Mother Gayle — they're the ones who saved Phil. It's barely possible that Sam Lester and I can claim a bit of credit, too. And as far as I'm concerned, Phil will stay right where he is until ready to leave in his own good time."

Dillon's retort was brusk.

"Your concern has nothing to do with it. Phil Ashland will leave your place when Colonel Gillem puts through the order to have him removed to the hospital at Fort Klamath. An ambulance wagon will be sent for him."

Ward Sebastian crossed his hands on his saddle horn and leaned forward slightly as he stared down at Dillon. The lines of his face had toughened, his eyes chilling and pinching down a trifle.

"You wouldn't be figuring on pulling strings to hurry the matter up, would you, Captain? If so, I suggest you go a little slow. Should he be moved before he is able to stand it, and suffers a setback, you'll be one damned unpopular man with the Ashland family."

Dillon's black eyes glinted. "When I or the Army needs your advice, Mister Sebastian, you'll be notified."

Sebastian straightened, scratched a sulphur match across his saddle horn, held it cupped in his hands while it fried from an acrid blue to a clear yellow flame and lighted his pipe, his weather-darkened cheeks caving inward as he puffed. Then his words fell, softly harsh.

"How the Army can afford such as you, Dillon, I'll never understand. God pity those who must serve under you!"

He touched his horse with the spur and rode off.

Back at the home ranch that evening, Sebastian faced Constance Ashland across the kitchen table, marveling at the resilience of this girl. Aside from a touch of shadow under her eyes and an equally faint suggestion of tautness about her lips, she was much her old self.

"It's off for Yreka in the morning," he told her. "If there is anything you need for yourself or Phil, I'll have Helen Chesbro fix it up for you."

Color stole through her cheeks at the intentness of his glance.

"Must you always be doing something for we Ashlands? And we already so deeply in your debt? Ward Sebastian, there would not be enough time in a thousand years for us to begin to repay you."

"I'm fully repaid just by you being here, and it will be rough to have you leave." He was still for a moment before adding gravely, "The ranch has always been a sort of refuge at the end of all the trails I travel. Yet I've never known the eagerness to return to it as now. Do you mind my saying that?"

"For saying something so nice? Of course not!"

The stirrings of a lonely man's hungers rose in him and he circled the table to stand tall and compelling before her. She held both her place and his glance, neither inviting or refusing. Her eyes were wells of flawless gray, holding neither coquetry or fear — just a simple demand for truth and nothing else. Truth in him and in herself.

Just now she was not certain of either. He saw this, and he turned away, searching for his pipe. Her words followed him softly.

"Thank you. I would not have either of us be anything less than very sure, Ward."

Breaking dawn, bleak and with the feel of snow in it. Out ahead the long line of pack mules, traveling at the fast half-walk, half-run pace of the trail when under empty saddles. Up at point, barely visible through the thinning mists of last night's murk, Sam Lester rode.

The steady shuffle and mutter of nimble hoofs, the small, muted noises of active saddle gear, the drift of warm animal odors, all these came back to Ward Sebastian, who found them familiar and good.

The threatened snow hit about midday, and by the time they reached Mike Golway's place had become a small blizzard. It seemed they might have to lay over for a time, but during the night the storm frittered out, and they went on the next morning through a world muffled in white.

In Yreka, Sebastian found Jeff and Helen Chesbro eager for firsthand news of the battle in the lava beds.

"There have been so many conflicting reports we don't know what to believe," Chesbro said. "One day the claim is that the troops won, the next it is that Kentipoos and his Modocs did."

"You can believe the last," Sebastian said. "In the words of my good friend, Major Ashland, we took a hell of a whipping."

"That bad, truly, Ward?" asked Helen Chesbro.

"That bad, Helen. Sam Lester and I volunteered for a spell of stretcher duty and saw a lot of the results, firsthand."

Jeff Chesbro shook a regretful head. "A bad business, no matter who wins. And Ward, Milo Biglow left word he'd like to see you, next time you came to town."

Sebastian frowned. "What would he want? Right now I'm hardly interested. Maybe after I clean up and eat I'll feel more generous."

198

Later, alone with him in her kitchen, Helen Chesbro watched him finish his supper.

"Do you, Ward?"

He looked at her. "Do I — what?"

"Feel more generous. I think you should go see Milo Biglow. And Anne, too."

"Why Anne?"

"Well, for goodness' sake! Harley Ritter is still around, you know."

"Fine! I wish both him and Anne luck."

Helen Chesbro stared at him. "That, Ward Sebastian, I do not understand!"

He got to his feet, took his coat from a wall peg, rummaged its pockets for his pipe. He considered soberly for a moment.

"It's really quite simple. There isn't a thing between Anne and me any more, Helen. There really never was. Nothing solid and enduring, I mean. Anne would never fit into my world, while I couldn't get along in hers. That understanding came to both of us the last time we were together."

"Well!" exclaimed Helen Chesbro again. "Does that leave me flat! And after all my careful scheming too. Would you mind telling me, Mister Sebastian, just what kind of girl would fit into your world?"

He grinned at her "You would have, if old Jeff hadn't got there first."

"Be serious!" she charged.

He got his pipe going before he answered.

"If you must know, she'd first have to understand my world and care for it the way I do. She'd be able to ride a long, rough trail with me and find reward for it in the purple sundown shadows and the warm goodness of a campfire in the dusk. She'd know the lure of star glitter and rejoice in all the flavors of the earth and in the things growing on it. She would fill a lonely ranch house with understanding and warmth so that it would never be lonely again. There's quite a bit more, but that gives the general picture. Now, Mrs. Chesbro, I hope you're content. For you've had from me thoughts I've kept mighty well guarded, up to now."

Helen Chesbro regarded him with lips parted and eyes bright with a gentle mischief.

"Ward Sebastian, you've left out the most important thing of all. Love! What's the matter? Are you, manlike, afraid of the word?"

"Along with the rest, don't you think that goes without saying?"

"Of course! I was just teasing. But I must say you've set up a pretty strenuous design for any girl to accomplish. Do you think you'll ever find such a wondrous creature?"

He shrugged a pair of big shoulders into his coat, while a twisted grin pulled at his mouth corners.

"Like old Tomas Iruga used to say — *quien sabe!*"

It was Milo Biglow who opened the door of the Biglow home at Ward Sebastian's knock, and reached for his hand.

"Heard you were in town, Ward, and have been waiting for you. Jeff Chesbro gave you the word?"

200

Sebastian nodded. "He did. Something in particular you wanted, sir?"

Before answering, Milo Biglow led the way into the living room, where he offered Sebastian a cigar and lighted one himself. After which he went into sober, contemplative thought for a time.

"I would have your opinion on something," he said finally. "You may have heard that General Canby is coming in to negotiate peace with the Modocs?"

"Yes."

"Very well." The faintest touch of pomposity came into Milo Biglow's manner. "I have been asked to serve as a member of a civilian peace commission to aid General Canby in his effort. Besides being close to the picture, you've also been an outspoken, realistic thinker on the problem. Therefore I'd like your opinion on the possibility of a satisfactory peace settlement."

Sebastian had been about to take a chair. Now he moved away from it, taking a couple of restless turns up and down the room. Abruptly he spoke.

"There is no possibility of it."

Milo Biglow frowned. "Surely you cannot be that positive?"

"I am. The Modocs will never consider a peace that does not guarantee them the right to return to their Lost River homeland and to remain there. And Washington will never agree to that reasonable solution. Any peace offered the Modoc will be based on the proposition that he consent to being corraled on some reservation far away from Lost River. So, at the very beginning there exists an unbreakable deadlock."

201

"General Canby is a very influential and convincing man," Biglow protested. "His word will carry a great deal of prestige."

Sebastian shrugged.

"In the eyes of the Modocs, General Canby and his commission, whoever they may be, and no matter how sincere their intentions, will be remorselessly judged by the lies and deceits of other white men in the past. Frankly, I doubt that now a meeting in good faith can be arranged with Captain Jack and his people."

"You hint at treachery?"

"Call it so," Sebastian said firmly. "They've experienced plenty of such from us, so it would only be natural for them to decide to give us some of the same in return. As I read the signs, everything points to a Modoc decision to fight this thing to a finish; even to virtual extinction for themselves. I tell you, anything can happen."

Milo Biglow buried his thoughts in a cloud of cigar smoke, and when he spoke his tone was subdued.

"In the lava-bed fighting we haven't fared too well, have we?"

"We've taken a complete and costly beating," Sebastian said bluntly. "And it's not too hard to believe that perhaps it is the inevitable price of some of our past misdeeds, now catching up with us."

Milo Biglow made a quick turn. "Ward, I've said you had a way of being pointedly realistic. Sometimes you are almost disagreeably so."

"Sorry, sir. But I never could see any sense in trying to deny facts."

202

"Facts," Biglow murmured. "I've considerable respect for them myself. But facing them can be a trifle upsetting at times. However, I appreciate your dropping in, Ward. Personally, I could stand a brandy. You'll join me?"

Milo Biglow poured the drinks then stood before the hearth, staring at the flames while he warmed his glass with his cupped hands. When he spoke, his words were barely audible, a man voicing his thoughts.

"There is little point or profit in being identified with a project foredoomed to failure. I believe I can best serve the future by remaining where I am. But — will Washington ever beckon again?"

He covered his doubt with brandy.

When, a little later, Ward Sebastian left, he carried conviction on two things. One was that there would be no serving on a peace commission by Milo Biglow. Another was that he would never hold the man in real respect again. For here was one who did not care to be identified with any cause — no matter what its worth — unless it be certain of success. So much, he thought cynically, for the self-righteous protestations of another proclaimed servant of the people.

At no time during the short evening had there been sign or mention of Anne. Yet Sebastian was certain she was in the house, because of the several lighted upstairs windows and because of his own trusted instincts.

Well, he knew no regret at not seeing her. In fact, when the Biglow door closed behind him for what he felt could very well be the last time, he knew but one reaction — one of freedom and relief.

CHAPTER
FOURTEEN

Back at the ranch, Sebastian found a relieved and happy household, with Phil Ashland sufficiently recovered to be propped up in bed and take interest in solid nourishment.

Kitty Dutra, her full dark beauty a soft and caressing thing, was ever at the bedside, and she and Phil had a way of looking at each other that closed out everyone else. Waiting his chance, Sebastian drew her aside.

"This, perhaps, I should have told you before, Kitty," he said gravely. "But with the concern over Phil I didn't want to add to the load. Now I will tell you."

She faced him steadily, her dark eyes intent. "What is it, Ward?"

"It seems I'm always bringing you the rough word. First, it was about Nick. Now it's your brother, Yance. He went into the lava-beds battle with some other civilian volunteers. He never came out, Kitty. But he died a damned good man."

She flinched slightly, a tinge of pallor flooding her cheeks. "You — you saw him?"

"And spoke with him. Neither he nor I realized it at the time, but that day Yance McCloud did his sister a great service. That day, though packing a mortal wound himself, Yance found Phil Ashland, when Phil was down and crying for water. And Yance gave Phil water he could have used himself, and so helped keep Phil alive until Sam and I came along with our stretcher. One big reason why that boy in the next room is with us, is because Yance McCloud measured up big when it counted. You can be proud of his memory, Kitty."

She wept softly. "Did he have — any word for me?"

"For you only and particularly. He asked that he be remembered and remembered well."

She turned away blindly. "He will be — he will be —!"

Later, subdued but calm, she was again at Phil Ashland's bedside, watching while he slept.

Out in the kitchen, Connie Ashland spoke to Sebastian ruefully.

"In a world all their own, those two. All I'm good for is to run errands and keep out of the way. And I can remember, not very long ago, when I was the cherished young sister, the main feminine concern in Phil's life. Now I'm a rank outsider."

Sebastian grinned. "I doubt it's that bad. You're just feeling a little too sorry for yourself."

"Perhaps," Connie admitted, smiling back at him. "I'm really very happy for both of them. Kitty is a grand person. I admit being doubtful at first, but no longer. For that matter," she went on, turning a little grave, "I find myself changing my opinion on a number of things. Realities, some of them very stark ones. For instance, *you* worry me."

"*I*! Worry you! In what way?"

"I'm remembering a man you spoke of once, and what your avowed intentions were toward him. A man named Provo Holt."

A touch of remoteness settled over Sebastian. His reply was guarded.

"I've seen nothing of him since the day I ran him off this ranch."

"Ah! But you will. There's an inevitability about some things, and I feel that way about this."

He studied her, trying to see past the warning look she'd thrown up. "What, I wonder, could such a worry mean?"

She shrugged enigmatically as she moved to leave the room. "Only what I said."

Off at daylight the following morning, Sebastian and Sam Lester were to rendezvous again with Bill Wiggin at Vinegar Spring, with more supplies for Homer Shadworth. But Wiggins was not at Vinegar Spring, so they went on, taking the long trail around the north end of the lake. Somewhere along this route, they figured to meet their man.

They made a camp at Peachtree and another at Boundary. They crossed Lost River at Natural Bridge on a gray and dismal morning in cold, driving rain, and found shelter at day's end in the house of the now-deserted ranch where Angus Laird and Obe Adams had been done to violent death on a red day which now seemed distant and almost unreal to Ward Sebastian.

Over a final pipe before seeking his blankets, he recalled the cruelty of that day and wondered what had become of Mary Laird and Lorna Adams; and of Mrs. Thurman and Mrs. Roblett.

During the night the rain ceased and they went on in the morning through a fog that billowed in off the lake. Later, when they climbed to a break in the Devil's Garden rim the gray overcast broke and the sun came through and the world steamed.

They met Bill Wiggin at the Blue Mountain camp, and learned he'd been held up by a chore for the military over past the Warners. They camped the night with him, saw him packed and away the next morning, then headed homeward once more, swinging wide to the southwest and a safe crossing through the lava beds by way of the old Lassen trail, well below the center of hostilities. Sebastian selected this route so he could contact Drury McVane at his mill on Firerock Creek, McVane's being a trading post for the wild country round about. He found Drury McVane avid for news and picked up a few frugal bits in return, as well as an idea of immediate supply needs.

"Provo Holt was supposed to come through at least three weeks ago with a whole string load for me," McVane said. "But he hasn't shown, and we're running damned short on everything. So, from now on, I say to hell with him! You meet my needs regular, Ward, I'll have no truck with Holt in the future. How soon can you come back with what I need?"

"Drury," Sebastian promised, "I'll be back next week."

"I'll be lookin' for you," McVane said.

The good weather lasted all the way home and, coming in across the final rims, Sebastian sensed a swelling vigor in the world around him and realized with a start that the season was speeding swiftly, with February fully gone and March partly so, and spring's first days only a little way off. When a man's days were fully of urgency and movement, he mused, time had a way of sliding by unnoticed.

Old Bob Gayle was waiting at the home corrals to help with the unsaddling chore. He looked at Sebastian guardedly, and his tone was almost too casual and matter-of-fact.

"Sure glad to have you fellers back. After all the company we've had for such a spell, Mother and me been findin' things a mite lonely, just bein' by ourselves again."

Sebastian had his head buried against a mule's shoulder while he worked at a sweat-sticky latigo. Now he came quickly around.

"What's that? You mean Miss Ashland and her brother are gone?"

"Kitty Dutra, too," nodded old Bob. "She went along with them. That biggity military feller, Cap'n Dillon, he come for them. Took 'em away in one of them ambulance wagons."

Sebastian stood silent, staring off into the shrouded distance of day's end. Disappointment was a knife's sharp edge, working in him. Coming through from Firerock Creek he had pushed the pack string hard, a growing eagerness driving him; eagerness for sight of Connie Ashland, and for the sound of her voice.

For the fact that this slender, gray-eyed girl had become the center of his world was a thing he no longer tried to deny to himself. He wasn't sure just when the conviction had come to him; perhaps it had been a gradual thing, with him hardly aware of it until, of a sudden, it was a fact fixed and certain. And now, with her gone, this world of his was sterile and empty.

He crossed to the house. Dusk, a blue tide, was coming in across the rims, and Mother Gayle had a light going in the kitchen. Busy at the stove, she turned as Sebastian came in. He closed the door, put the width of his shoulders against it, and his voice ran low and deep.

"When did they leave?"

"Four days ago," Mother Gayle told him. Reading the shadowed, baffled disappointment in his eyes, she quickly added: "Connie left this for you."

She took an envelope from a kitchen shelf, then turned to the stove again while he spread the enclosure on the table by the lamp. Just the faintest hint of a fragrance lifted to him. The writing was as clean lined and graceful as the girl who had penned it.

Ward:

Jud Dillon has come with an ambulance wagon and escort, and the official order for Phil's removal to medical quarters at Fort Klamath. I must, of course, go along. Kitty Dutra is accompanying us, as both Phil and I would not have it otherwise. Personally, I would have preferred to wait until Phil was a little stronger, but the Army has its own way of doing things, against which it is useless to argue. Of late I find myself growing a little resentful of that fact.

How much we all owe you! And now we must run off this way, and I feel very guilty about it. Also there are other emotions loose in me, too disturbing and uncertain to put in writing.

They are waiting for me. Oh, Ward, these are such strained and treacherous days, how can we be sure of anything? Only, I find that in closing, I must say this. There is a great gentleness in my heart for you.

Connie.

How very empty and still was the house! And it would do no good to listen for her step or the sound of her voice.

There was another note for him, a short one, in Kitty Dutra's unformed scrawl.

When you brought me to your ranch, Ward, you said it would give me the chance to find a new faith in life. I have found all of that and so much more I'll never cease blessing you.

Kitty.

Spring came in on the wings of a storm which battered the country for five days, leaving creeks and rivers roaring full and the snow banked deep and treacherous above the higher mountain trails.

Calamity hit two of Jeff Chesbro's pack outfits. One, caught in a slide in Cloudy Pass, lost a packer and ten mules out of eighteen. Another, also on the way in from Crescent City on the coast, ran into swift-rising storm waters at a Klamath River ford and lost exactly half of a twenty-four animal string.

Good to his promise, Ward Sebastian had returned to Firerock Creek and McVane's Mill with a loaded string. Caught there by the storm he had to lay over with McVane until the weather broke. When it did, Firerock Creek was a torrent and it was necessary to wait two more impatient days before the water dropped far enough for a safe crossing. So it was that a full two weeks passed from the time Sebastian left Yreka until he got back to hear of Jeff Chesbro's crippling loss.

He did not hesitate a moment in placing his string at Jeff's need.

"I'll have to head down into the big valley of the Sacramento for more mules," Chesbro said ruefully, "and I don't know when I'll get back with them. Helen and Ben Stiles can run the store all right, and if you could make a trip or two across to Crescent City for me, Ward —?"

"A dozen, if necessary," Sebastian said. "You go get those mules."

As though relenting after striking such a harsh blow, the weather turned benevolent and full of the warming vigor of spring. However, with a stretch of the trail washed out here, and blocked by a slide there, travel through to Crescent City was slow and tiring. Streams were still high, and fording the larger ones tricky and

211

dangerous. So it was a worn-down string of pack animals that finally plodded into quarters here in this mistshrouded coastal town where the Pacific's gray rollers boomed against the headlands and the gulls mewed plaintively in the fog.

April was ten days old before Sebastian started back to Yreka. It was fifteen by the time he arrived there. The town was seething, and it was Helen Chesbro, while she served him supper, who gave him the cause.

"The Modocs have done murder again, Ward. They met with a peace commission for a talk, and then, even as the talk was under way, drew guns and began shooting. They killed General Canby and another member of the commission and badly wounded a third. The word is that it was Captain Jack himself who shot General Canby. Why should they do such a thing, Ward? Why such madness? Why, why?"

Sebastian brooded for a little time. Then he shrugged.

"Old and bitter wrongs, long remembered, Helen. Such things live with all men, red or white. Under similar conditions white men cold-bloodedly slaughtered Captain Jack's father; the Ben Wright affair, you remember? We've written a lot of other dirty rules in this game of grab and destroy. How can we, in full conscience, blame the Modoc for using a few of them? A sad, sad thing, but —!" He shrugged again.

"What will happen now?" Helen Chesbro asked.

"Just a hastening of the inevitable end," Sebastian told her. "I'm sorry for our future certain dead — and for theirs."

212

General Canby's death, and the manner of it, brought immediate grim orders to Colonel Gillem from Washington. No further attempt to treat with the Modoc would be made. He was to be fought to the death or to utter surrender. Kentipoos — Captain Jack — was to be brought in, dead or alive. And new attack on the lava stronghold was to begin immediately.

On the seventeenth of April, Ward Sebastian and Sam Lester left Yreka on a second trip to Crescent City. On the eighteenth, after seventy-two hours of savage fighting, during which the lava stronghold of the Modocs was heavily pounded with mortar shells by artillery units that had arrived on the scene, forces attacking from two sides at once finally achieved junction along the lake shore, thus cutting the Modocs off from their water supply. That night Captain Jack and his people slipped away like ghosts, leaving the shell-battered stronghold for the weary troopers to occupy next day.

On the trail, Sebastian heard nothing of this, nor, while in Crescent City with April's end just four days distant, of the Thomas and Wright massacre, when troops under the two-named officers were ambushed deep in the lavas and almost annihilated.

But he was back in Yreka, early in May, when word of the battle of Dry Lake came in, telling of the disastrous defeat the Modocs had taken at the hands of the dogged, determined long-suffering military. Later advices told that following their Dry Lake defeat, the Modocs had broken up into small bands and scattered to the four winds. And this, Sebastian knew, meant that now the final end was not far off.

Jeff Chesbro, with two new packers helping, came back from the big valley of the Sacramento with thirty head of pack mules.

"Less than half of what I need," he told Sebastian, "but I got a man lining up some more, and expect them along inside another month."

Sebastian, free again now to take care of his own obligations and mindful of the needs of Bill Wiggin for Surprise Valley, made up his loads and took the old and well-remembered trail to the east for the first time in long weeks. Riding it now, marking every familiar mile of it, he mused on how a land once thoroughly known and lived with and traveled across, could lay its claim on a man.

For some it might be the timbered hills, or the sloping valley or the flat and open plains, with each man free to his choice. But for him it must always be this land of distant, lonely buttes, of curving lava rims with the rich, hidden basins in between.

For him the pocketed aspens, the colorful blankets of cherry brush, the gaunt limbed cedars and compact junipers, and the long-running thickets of mahogany. For him the strong green of spring's verdant grass in the sheltered basins, where the wild flowers splashed their warm beauty below the rims, and where the marmot fed and whistled his bright greeting to the sun. All this, and to the south, immaculate against the sky, the mountain.

Shasta!

His world. He thought of another day along this same trail, and of the girl who had ridden a stretch of it with him. A girl who saw, all round about, the same things to exult in that he did. A girl who had stepped abruptly into this world of his, and, just as abruptly, stepped out of it, leaving it bleakly empty for him. Yes, there had been a note. But since then, no word, no sign.

At the home ranch there was a message from Bill Wiggin.

"He was here and waited around as long as he could," reported Bob Gayle. "But he'd agreed to a run up to Fort Klamath for the military and had to leave to take care of that. But he said he'd be at the Blue Mountain camp in the Devil's Garden around the first of the month."

"We'll meet him there," Sebastian nodded.

They laid over at the ranch for several days, resting up the pack string and repairing worn equipment. Then they left in time to meet Bill Wiggin, as promised on the first of June at the Blue Mountain camp. Around the fire they swapped trail gossip and Wiggin came up with one item which tightened Ward Sebastian's jaw and narrowed his eyes.

"We got competition shapin' up on the Surprise Valley trade," Wiggin said. "Atwood and Carter are reachin' out from Linkville, accordin' to what I heard comin' through from Fort Klamath. And who do you think they got lined up to run a string for them? Provo Holt. Yes, sir. I saw Holt and a half-breed helper gettin' a string ready for the first trip. Man, you'd think Ray

Atwood and Charley Carter could get somebody more reliable than Provo Holt."

Sam Lester spat into the fire. "I was hopin' Provo Holt had either fell off a high hill or into a deep hole by this time."

"No such luck," grumbled Wiggin. "His kind just keep on clutterin' up a good world and causin' trouble."

Ward Sebastian stirred restlessly, his thoughts reaching farther than to Linkville.

"How were things at Fort Klamath, Bill?"

"Lot of military comin' and goin'. They figger the big ruckus is about done with. They got the Modocs split up, a few here, a few there, and runnin' more of them down every day. Talk was they figger to round up Captain Jack himself most any time, now."

The bearded packer sucked at his pipe in silence for a little time before going on.

"Saw Nick Dutra's widow up at Klamath. She sure looked fine and pretty. I talked some with her. She's set to marry up with a young officer who was wounded in that first big lava-beds fight, and she was just singin' happy about it, so I was glad for her too. I allus did like Kitty Dutra."

Later in the evening, with Bill Wiggin snoring in his blankets, Ward Sebastian crouched by the fire, silent over a pipe long gone cold. Beside him, Sam Lester finally spoke abruptly.

"You got a lick of sense, you'll head for Forth Klamath first thing in the mornin'."

216

Sebastian turned his head, met Sam's shrewd, puckered glance.

"So?"

"Wise old fox, eh?"

Sam shrugged. "Constance Ashland ain't been out of your mind since the night she caught up with us at Mike Golway's place. Not that I blame you any, understand, for there's one girl who's the pure quill."

"And she's been Army all her life," Sebastian said gravely. "She's not the sort to change easy."

"How do you know about that unless you go find out?" Sam demanded. "Boy, come mornin', you get the hell out of here. With no loads to wrastle, I can take the string back to the ranch by myself."

Sebastian stood up, prowled about the fading fire coals a couple of times before pausing to stare out across the night. Finally he nodded and spoke softly.

"All right, Sam. Tomorrow I ride!"

With no pack string in front of him, Sebastian traveled fast, his horse strong in morning's chill. He held to a line a little west of north, figuring to break past the Oregon Rim of the Devil's Garden before turning more strongly west for Linkville and Fort Klamath beyond. Now that his decision was made, he knew a buoyant eagerness, and began wishing back the miles.

He rode through timber stands of varying extent and across wide flats of open country where new grass lay emerald under the stunted sage. He circled heavy thickets of mahogany and matted stands of jackpines. Over beyond the distant Warner Mountains the sun crawled up and peered at him, pressing its warmth across his shoulders.

Toward midmorning he rode through a ragged fringe of timber and faced a stretch of open that in summer would be a dry flat, but which now held a shallow film of water, spiked with scattered clumps of grass. Above one spot where a small hump of muddy earth showed, a flight of swallows fluttered and twittered.

But it wasn't sight of the flight of swallows that caused Sebastian to set his horse up sharply and swing back into the timber; it wasn't sight of anything. It was sound, the quick, ragged rattle of gunfire, somewhere out past the spread of surface water.

Leaning a little in his saddle, Sebastian listened, at the same time sliding his rifle from the scabbard under his knee and laying the weapon across the saddle in front of him. As nearly as he could tell, perhaps a dozen shots had made up that burst of firing. Certainly more than one gun. But why the shooting and at what?

A moment later he got partial answer. From a fringe of mahogany brush broke a pack animal under full load. It splashed out into the water, slowed to a stop and stood spread-legged and with sagging head. Abruptly its knees caved and it went heavily down, to kick once or twice, then go shrunken and still.

Came further sound from beyond the mahoganies where a belt of timber lifted. Out there a man set up a wild, high crying, a sound carrying pain and terror. It struck a peak of hoarse agony, then broke sharply off into a throbbing silence.

Watching, listening, Ward Sebastian waited, waited through long minutes. He heard nothing more and saw only what had been there before, the down and now dead pack mule yonder, and the flitting, twittering swallows. This was a hard thing to interpret, and his mind picked at it warily.

When he did stir his horse to movement again it was in a circling move, following the shelter of a timber fringe which curved around the western end of the water flat. Here the forest mold lay deep and moistly soft and it muffled sound and movement. And here Sebastian again glimpsed something other than a world as it should be.

A spot of color lay at the edge of a jackpine thicket, color once white, but now the gray of a weather-bleached canvas tarpaulin. Under the tarp was a pack, and under the pack the crumpled bulk of a second mule, a dark and drying smear of blood showing on its side where a bullet had entered.

Now the answer was clear. Somewhere not greatly distant, a pack train had been ambushed. This mule, shot through the lungs, had stampeded this far before going down, drowning in its own blood. The one back in the water flat, with just as mortal, though not so swiftly fatal a wound, had made it a little farther.

Here was a wanton business, shooting pack animals in this way; wanton business by wanton minds, lost and desperate and no longer caring.

Sebastian rode cautiously on until the acrid tang of wood smoke struck his nostrils. For a moment he stayed in the saddle, standing high in his stirrups as he

219

tested the drift. Then he swung down, dropped the reins and went ahead on foot, rifle poised and ready.

Abruptly he saw them. Three of them. Ragged, shaggy-headed figures, crouched over a small, smoldering fire, gnawing at greasy chunks of half-cooked bacon. A little way from them a third pack mule lay dead, the load of this one ripped open and a miscellany of food supplies scattered around.

Two of those dark, wild figures, Sebastian knew by sight and name. The third was a Modoc he had never seen before. All three were too intent on their ravenous gobbling of bacon to guess his approach, and he worked up to within thirty yards of them before lifting his rifle to his shoulder and hitting out at them with his harsh call.

"You, Barncho — Black Jim —!"

They came up and around like startled animals. It was the one Sebastian did not recognize who recovered first and caught up the rifle lying at his feet. The intent was plain and there could be but one reply. Sebastian shot him to death with the dispassionate detachment of cold necessity.

Barncho and Black Jim had stacked their rifles against a nearby tree, and there was no mistaking the desperate purpose in their black, wild eyes. Sebastian swung the lever of his rifle, jacking a fresh shell home.

"You're dead if you try it!"

For a breath they were as taut and dangerous as panthers, eyes glittering. Then, as abruptly as a snuffed flame, all fight went out of them and they hunkered down, side by side, seeming to shrink until they were just a pair of incredibly dirty, half-starved, blank-faced figures.

There was something fatalistic in their attitude, as if they had considered within themselves and decided that here was the certain end as they had known it must come. They had done their best, killing the white man and destroying his possessions. But now their world was gone and they must go with it.

They offered no sign of resistance when Sebastian motioned them apart and tied them up with rope from the rifled pack. Yes, he knew these two, Barncho and Black Jim, and he knew that they knew him. But he could wring no answering words or sign from them. The feeling grew that he was dealing with something completely alien, with physical shells empty of human reaction; that though he had captured the substance, the spirit had eluded him.

Their guns, and that of the dead Modoc, he beat to uselessness against a tree. He went back after his horse, then began his search. Not far away he found the first sprawled figure, a half-breed packer who had been shot twice and lay as a man asleep, face resting on one doubled up arm.

Farther along was another, a man who had been savagely treated before done to final death.

Provo Holt. Lying dead and disfigured there under the softly stirring, sun-glided timber.

Sebastian, having known this man so bitterly well in life, recognized him now in the bitterness of violent death.

Provo Holt.

Sebastian recalled a day at Desolation Flat and the terrified hopelessness of the young squaw and mother who had died there by Provo Holt's gun. Well, he mused bleakly, she was fully avenged now, and by her own kind, which was fitting.

He found two more dead pack mules and located ten uninjured ones scattered about through the timber, as well as the two saddle mounts Provo Holt and his packer had been using.

He stripped the packs from the sound mules, unsaddled the animals and turned them loose. The packs he stacked about the trunk of a pine, spread and roped down tarpaulins over the pile. The chipmunks were certain to be about their small mischief, and other wild marauders might strike, but, Sebastian concluded, it was the best he could do. If Atwood and Carter moved fast enough, they'd be able to salvage the most of it. The mules, while certain to drift some, could be tracked down and rounded up again.

He had more definite use for the two saddle mounts. He tied Barncho into the saddle of one and Black Jim into that of the other, and then, with the two horses following at fast lead, drove on for Linkville.

CHAPTER
FIFTEEN

Spring at its fullest spread its benevolence over Fort Klamath, and to Connie Ashland it was as if prison gates had been opened. To walk again in the sun, to lift one's face to its brightness and warmth was a full and rewarding pleasure, and for the first time since leaving Ward Sebastian's ranch, some semblance of her old verve for life came back to her.

Sheer contrast made her recall the trip up to Fort Klamath with her brother Phil and Kitty Dutra, a trip that remained a dreary miserable experience, what with its discomfort and her worry over Phil in his weakened condition. For the big storm had caught them well north of Linkville, and when they reached the Sprague River ford, raging waters made a crossing impossible. So in the dark and dripping shelter of a timber patch they had waited out the days, cramped and miserable, wet and cold.

It had been bad enough cooped up inside the ambulance wagon, but at least it offered some shelter. The troopers of the escort detail, however, took dreary punishment in their makeshift camp. Now, even though it was all weeks gone, and today the sun shone warmly across a broad land sweetened and enriched with winter's rain and swelling strong with all the promise of spring's fecundity, she could not completely rid herself of the edge of bitterness that trip had awakened in her.

Considerable activity held the fort these days, with troops returning from the lava-beds battlefield, now that resistance by the Modoc had been broken and scattered, and with the end of the uneven struggle in sight. Commanding one group of returning troops was Major Ross Ashland.

Stirred by emotional crosscurrents she did not altogether understand, Connie wept a little on her uncle's shoulder. Now she had the two men of her family safely with her again. But for how long?

Throughout the fort there was much talk of increasingly serious Sioux trouble in the Dakota Territory, and of the growing restiveness of the Apache in the Southwest. It was a certainty that fresh orders for many would soon come through, for these were blooded troops, now. And wherever such orders might take Phil, Kitty would be with him, for their marriage was just short weeks distant. So, for Connie, every day had increased her feeling of being an outsider.

The returning troops brought prisoners with them; dark ragged figures, moving with the funereal tread of hopelessness.

"You got to feel sorry for the poor devils," Major Ashland said. "No braver battle than theirs was ever fought. Less than sixty of them against all our hundreds. I tell you, Connie, there is little about our victory to take pride in. I'm afraid my sentiments in this affair are pretty much the same as Ward Sebastian's."

224

Connie showed a slight hesitancy. "Have you seen anything of Ward, Uncle Ross?"

"Not since the day he brought me word of Phil having passed the crisis. You —?"

Connie shook her head, turning away to hide the swift new start of tears, and furious with herself because of them. Sometimes, of late, she felt she almost hated Ward Sebastian.

Of course she had left the ranch while he was away, but that was not her fault. That was the Army. And she had left a note in which she had expressed some pretty revealing sentiments. To which there had been no answer at all . . .

The passing days brought little betterment in her mood. She rejoiced with Phil and Kitty in their happiness, but when considering her own future she grew pensive, knowing a sharp and ever deepening sense of aloneness.

Captain Judson Dillon caught her in the depths of this mood one day as she stood in the doorway of her quarters, looking out across the limits of the fort and seeing none of it.

"Connie, would you be feeling sorry for yourself?"

She flashed him a quick glance. "Perhaps."

"Over what?"

She shrugged. "I see so little in my future to cheer about."

He seized on the opening swiftly.

"Your future is something I've long wanted to discuss with you. You know how I feel about you. I'd like to know — have you ever considered me?"

225

"Yes," she admitted, with blunt and disconcerting frankness, "I have. And it wouldn't work out, Jud. My heart wouldn't be in it, and where I fail to love deeply, no substitute could ever do."

A dark flush rushed across his thinly handsome features. "What have you against me?"

"I've nothing against you, Jud. It isn't a question of anything like that at all. It's merely the proposition of loving or not loving. As honest individuals we cannot help our feelings in such things. Also, I'm up against a way of life I no longer care for."

Jud Dillon blinked. "I'm afraid I don't know just what you mean. I'll do anything to make you happy. You know that."

She came around to face him fully. "Very well. If I agreed to marry you, Jud, would you resign your commission?"

He stared, astounded. "Resign my commission! What do you mean?"

"Just that. Would you?"

"Good Lord, Connie, do you realize what you're asking? I'm a professional soldier. My career is my life. What kind of a harsh bargain would you drive?"

"Don't worry," she said gently, dropping a hand on his arm, "it won't be necessary. I merely brought up such an unthinkable possibility to show you why there could be no happiness for us, either way. For should you resign your commission at my request, you'd end up despising me, and I wouldn't blame you. On the other hand, I'm no longer content with Army life. I'm

226

no longer willing to accept the weight of its never-ending authority."

"Girl, what are you thinking about? All your life you've been Army. You couldn't leave it now."

"Oh, but I could!" she retorted. "I've seen something of a wild, free land, Jud, and the wonderful freedom of it has infected me. I know I could never be wholly happy again in the restrictive monotony of an Army post. For, no matter its size or location, the weight of inevitable authority is always present, and I find myself increasingly restive under it."

"But," argued Dillon desperately, "there's Phil and your Uncle Ross. What will they say? You can't turn away from them."

"I'm not turning away from them. And I've nothing against Army life for those who like it. They are good for it and it is good for them. And I'm truly thankful that there are men like you and Phil and Uncle Ross and all the other professionals of all rank and grade. For without you, this country of ours would be in sad shape. Yes, Jud, I'm well aware of all such things. But I also know I'm not the same person who came up into this country a few months ago. I can't help the change in me, and I'm not sorry over it."

Movement in the lower area of the fort drew Connie's glance. Another file of troops coming in, trail- and battle-worn. A couple more prisoners with them. Also a civilian, a big-shouldered man who loomed high in his saddle. Connie stepped swiftly past Captain Judson Dillon, one soft, wholly eager word on her lips.

"Ward!"

For a moment Jud Dillon watched her, half angry in the knowledge that he'd ceased to exist in this girl's consciousness. Then he accepted the inevitable. Army training and its code had its way with him. Arrow-straight he walked to meet Ward Sebastian, who had reined in and dismounted.

"Captain," Sebastian said, "how are you? Could you tell me where I might find Miss Ashland?"

Captain Dillon made an indicating turn of his head. "In her quarters, yonder." And now Jud Dillon fulfilled the code in its very best tradition. He put out his hand. "I'm glad to see you, Sebastian."

"Captain," Sebastian said, as their palms met, "if there be apologies due on my part for things said or done in the past, consider them rendered."

He went on then and she met him in the doorway of her quarters. She tried to keep her tone light.

"Hello, Ward. What brings you here?"

He regarded her gravely. "You know, Connie."

He was hard-jawed and travel-stained and he seemed to fill the whole of this small room with his big-shouldered presence. Facing him, Connie's gray eyes blurred and a treacherous quaver crept into her voice.

"You might have answered my note. There were dispatch riders coming and going constantly between here and the Tule Lake headquarters. Why — why didn't you?"

"You said you needed time to be sure."

"And — and you?"

"Would I be here, otherwise?"

228

The tears brimmed over as she went into the strong comfort of his arms.

"I — I've been so lonely, Ward. And I'm sure — so very sure!"

Some time later there was sudden commotion in the lower fort area, and a thin, hard shout carried electrifying word.

"Kentipoos! Captain Jack! They captured him on Willow Creek. They're bringing in Captain Jack!"

Up and down the word spread. From all quarters officers and men appeared, hurrying. This prisoner they had to see, for this was the big one.

Kentipoos! Captain Jack!

He moved with his captors to the stockade. Just a ragged, squatty figure, yet at this moment he walked with the great height of unshakable dignity, and the shadow he threw was long and wide. His dark face was gaunt and sadly stoic, his black eyes deep sunken. Eyes that looked straight ahead, fixed unwaveringly on the far, fathomless distances of eternity. Silent himself, he was now suddenly paid the tribute of silence.

Kentipoos, the Modoc! Captain Jack!

Ward Sebastian spoke softly.

"He has the same look about him that Barncho and Black Jim showed me. They've captured the substance of him, but his spirit has slipped away."

Standing in the circle of Sebastian's arm, Connie Ashland asked:

"What will they do with him, Ward?"

"The word I've had is that all directly responsible for General Canby's death must hang. Which will be a senseless, useless thing. For you cannot punish something that has moved beyond your reach."

Connie shivered, pressed her face against his shoulder.

"The mountain — Shasta. He'll never see it again."

"Never," Sebastian told her, his voice going gruff in his throat. "And all Kentipoos ever asked was just simple justice!"

MODOC, THE LAST SUNDOWN

W...   A man
wi...   And it
lo...   ast . . .
To...   1 their
an...   hated
wl...   or their
pl...   the
co...   traitor
to...   for the
M...   eks to
pr...   e one
ob...   lan. To
all...   s guns
an...